STAR WARS

LAST OF THE JEDI

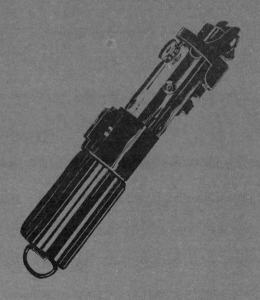

MASTER OF DECEPTION
BY JUDE WATSON

SCHOLASTIC INC.

New York Toronto London Auckland Sydney Mexico City New Delhi Hong Kong Buenos Aires

ISBN-13: 978-0-439-68142-1
ISBN-10: 0-439-68142-1

12 11 10 9 8 7 6 5 4 3   8 9 10 11 12 13/0

Printed in the U.S.A.   40
First printing, February 2008

GUIDE TO CHARACTERS

Obi-Wan Kenobi: the great Jedi Master; now in exile on Tatooine

Ferus Olin: former Jedi Padawan and apprentice to Siri Tachi; now a double-agent working for the Empire in order to undermine it wherever he can

Solace: formerly the Jedi Knight Fy-Tor Ana; became a bounty hunter after the Empire was established

Garen Muln: weakened by long months of hiding after Order 66; resides on the secret asteroid base that Ferus Olin has established

Ry-Gaul: on the run since Order 66; found by Solace

THE ERASED

A loose confederation of those who have been marked for death by the Empire who give up their official identities and disappear; centered on Coruscant

Dexter Jettster: former owner of Dex's Diner; establishes a safehouse in Coruscant's Orange District

Oryon: former head of a prominent Bothan spy network during the Clone Wars; divides his time between Ferus's secret asteroid base and Dex's hideout

Keets Freely: former award-winning investigative journalist targeted for death by the Empire; now hiding out in Dex's safehouse

Curran Caladian: former Senatorial aide from Svivreni and cousin to Tyro Caladian, the deceased Senatorial aide and friend to Obi-Wan Kenobi; marked for death due to his outspoken resistance to the establishment of the Empire; lives in Dex's safehouse

GUIDE TO
CHARACTERS

KEEPERS OF THE BASE

Raina: renowned pilot from the Acherin struggle against the Empire

Toma: former general and commander of the resistance force on Acherin

THE ELEVEN

Resistance movement on Bellassa beginning to be known throughout the Empire. First established by eleven men and women but grown to include hundreds in the city of Ussa and more supporters planet-wide.

Roan Lands: one of the original Eleven; friend and partner to Ferus Olin; killed by Darth Vader

Dona Telamark: a supporter of the Eleven; hid Ferus Olin in her mountain retreat after his escape from an Imperial prison

Wil: part of the original Eleven; now its lead coordinator

Dr. Amie Antin: loaned her medical services to the group, then joined later; now the second-in-command but also spying as a doctor in the EmPal SuRecon on Coruscant

GUIDE TO
CHARACTERS

Trever Flume: Ferus Olin's thirteen-year-old companion; former street kid and black market operator on Bellassa; now an honorary member of the Bellassan Eleven and a resistance fighter presently on Coruscant on a secret mission

Clive Flax: former musician; corporate spy turned double agent during the Clone Wars; friend to Ferus and Roan; escaped with Ferus from the Imperial prison world of Dontamo

Astri Oddo: formerly Astri Oddo Divinian; left the politician Bog Divinian after he joined with Sano Sauro and the Separatists; now on the run hiding from Bog; expert slicer specializing in macro-frame computer code systems

Lune Oddo Divinian: Force-adept eight-year-old; son of Astri and Bog Divinian; now hidden on a secret asteroid base under the tutelage of Garen Muln

Linna Naltree and Tobin Gantor: husband and wife; friends of Jedi Ry-Gaul

Flame: mysterious and wealthy friend to the Eleven and other resistance groups; now on Coruscant

Breha, Queen of Alderaan: wife of Bail Organa and adoptive mother of Leia; daughter of Padmé Amidala and Anakin Skywalker

Bail Organa: husband of Breha and adoptive father of Leia; a Senator on Alderaan

Hydra: head of the Empire's evil Inquisitors

Jenna Zan Arbor: an evil scientist employed by the Empire; working on an anti-memory drug on Coruscant

CHAPTER ONE

Bail Organa stood at the window and watched his daughter Leia run through the gardens. Every day she learned new skills and grew steadier on her feet. His wife, Breha, sat cross-legged on the grass, laughing as Leia picked flowers.

Bail found that he was holding his breath. He let it out slowly.

They had thought the incident was nothing. An accident averted, nothing more than that. Leia had been with one of her caregivers, Memily, who worked in the kitchen but also volunteered to help out with the children. They had gone to a park at the other end of the city of Aldera to play, somewhere Leia had never been before. The park ended in high sandstone bluffs that overlooked the sea. There were fences along the perimeter, cleverly designed in a latticework that looked like white branches but were actually durasteel.

Except one of the areas was weakened, and Memily had been about to lean against it to admire the view.

Bail still wasn't sure exactly what had happened. Memily had told him the story, still shaken from the experience. She'd sworn that Leia, who was not yet a year old, had suddenly twisted her head and thrown her laserball directly at the spot. The laserball had hit the fence, which had shook so hard that Memily had been warned of its instability.

Perhaps Memily wouldn't have fallen. Perhaps the fence would have held. Perhaps Leia had just randomly thrown the laserball.

Recounting this, Memily had fixed Bail with her large dark eyes. She was a young woman from the country, still a bit cowed by the atmosphere at the royal palace. "It was like she *knew*, sir," she'd said. "Like she saw something before it happened. I saw it in her eyes. Then she smiled at me and . . . kept on playing."

Memily was completely trustworthy; everyone in Bail's palace was. All those who lived on the grounds were either family or were related to the family's most trusted allies. Memily was the daughter of an old friend. Bail knew that she would have never talked about the incident to anyone but him.

But somehow this tiny incident, this minuscule ripple in the middle of an ordinary day, had been reported to the Empire.

Someone had seen it, and someone had talked, and

maybe that person had told the story at the spaceport, a place from which someone might have taken it back to Coruscant. Spies were everywhere now. The Empire paid handsomely for the merest scraps of information. So someone, at some point, had thought that the Empire might be interested in word of a child with amazing reflexes.

Imperial informers were now a part of life in the galaxy, Bail supposed, but he didn't believe there were any on Alderaan. The society here was too close-knit, and everyone was bitterly opposed to the new Imperial order. It was just bad luck that the news had gone so far . . . all the way to the Imperial Inquisitors.

Bad luck. Was that it? A Jedi wouldn't say so. A Jedi would say that the dark side of the Force now moved through the galaxy, tempting some, encouraging others to exercise their worst impulses.

The good news was that nobody knew that the child was Leia. There was just a report of a child, neither male nor female, and a caregiver who had quickly hustled her away. He couldn't fault Memily for that, but it had attracted attention.

Bail glanced around the room, at the transparisteel doors that marched along one entire wall, so that the gardens would be seen in full display. Leia called this room the "inside-outside room." The palace had always been an open place. That was the Alderaan way. Any citizen could come to the door and knock. Bail had security placed here during the Clone Wars, but it was minimal. Breha had fought him even about that. She would not change her planet's traditions for the sake of a repellent regime, she said, her chin lifted in that way he knew so well.

She was right, actually. If the Empire wanted access to this place, they would get in no matter how much security he ordered.

Now two Imperial Inquisitors were due to arrive later that day. He had told Breha to take Leia away for the duration. He could see them now, heading toward the private gates the family used to enter and exit the official palace compound. Bail felt better knowing that Leia wouldn't be at home.

Not that an Inquisitor would pick up anything strange. Leia was a normal toddler. Advanced for her age, yes, but he'd never seen any evidence of Force sensitivity in her. He had hoped, instead, that whatever she had inherited from her true parents had been all from Padmé. Her intelligence, her courage, perhaps some of her grace . . . not just her brown eyes.

Yet part of Anakin Skywalker was there, too. Bail had hoped it wouldn't be. In this galaxy, ability with the Force would be a burden to his child, not a gift.

So much to hide, Bail thought. The Inquisitors would come, and they would walk the city, and they would comb through records, and they would invade the privacy of the citizens of Alderaan, and if Bail had anything to do about it, they would find nothing and leave. The report of a toddler with an amazing pitching arm would be tossed aside, as well it should, lost among the millions of tips the Imperial investigators received from those trying to curry favor, trying to move up in the system.

Bail sighed. He would have to cooperate. But he wasn't about to make it easy.

CHAPTER TWO

Ferus Olin resisted the urge to tug at the collar of his Inquisitor's robe. To him the robe was unnecessarily ominous-looking. The hoods were designed to conceal the face. He had remarked to his fellow Inquisitor, Hydra, that it seemed counter-productive to wear such a frightening costume if you were trying to coax information out of reluctant subjects, but Hydra had merely stared at him with her flat, expressionless gaze and said, "The Empire does not coax."

Right. He knew he should really pay attention to this new Imperial lingo. They didn't coax, they didn't ask, they didn't defer, they didn't take into account that anyone they came in contact with was in fact a living, breathing creature. Ruthless efficiency was the only way to go.

Ferus hated being a double agent. If the Emperor hadn't given him this particular job, he would have dropped away and gone back to the resistance. But given the chance to head up the Inquisitors who were tracking down rumors of Force-adepts, he couldn't turn it down. If he could locate them, he could save them. And if locating them took being an Inquisitor for awhile, he would do it.

But this robe . . . he'd been in two Imperial prisons so far and this robe felt like the third.

If it hadn't been for Obi-Wan Kenobi, he wouldn't be on Alderaan at all. All that solitude was making Obi-Wan even more of a mystery man than usual. Obi-Wan had his secrets, and he was keeping them. That didn't stop him, however, from issuing edicts to Ferus every once in awhile. When Ferus had listed the Force-sensitive prospects, for some reason this nameless toddler on Alderaan had gotten Obi-Wan's attention.

Imperial Inquisitor Hydra sat beside him, her expression neutral. She never said a word if she didn't have to. Her hood shadowed her face, and it was rare that he caught a glimpse of her expression. She didn't seem to have an emotion about anything. They'd traveled together for two days now, and she had never complained about delays or bad food or the faulty engine light that had grounded them for five hours at a decrepit spaceport.

She piloted the airspeeder, zooming through the space lanes of Aldera without regard to anyone else. The palace lay on a slight rise at the edge of the city, overlooking the vast lake. It was a gracious complex of buildings surrounded by gardens and orchards. Terraces on various levels afforded the inhabitants plenty of air and light in Alderaan's temperate climate. Hydra brought the airspeeder down, releasing the repulsorlift motor so that the airspeeder crushed a plot of clover.

Ferus gathered himself for the encounter. Bail Organa was a personal hero of his. He had followed Organa's career in the Senate, heard his speeches, read his writings. His passion for justice was never an occasion for ego or grandstanding; his quiet resolve was, for Ferus, the essence of what a politician should be and rarely was.

And Bail would despise him.

Not only was he entering his house as an enemy, but Bail no doubt knew his background. He would accept the official Imperial line that Ferus had been a great hero of the Bellassan resistance before seeing the error of his ways and joining the Empire. In other words, Bail would see him as a traitor to every ideal he held dear.

Ferus and Hydra approached the palace and walked through the gates. Ferus was surprised at the lack of security. It had to be there, but he sensed no hidden alarms or sensors. No weapons were allowed on Alderaan, but still, he would have expected some sort of protection for the Queen and her large extended family.

They followed a winding path through ancient trees with thick trunks of dark golden wood. The gardens were in bloom, and all the flowers were bursts of color against the dense dark greens of the foliage.

The path led them to a wide front door that was intricately carved from what looked like the massive trunk of one of the majestic trees that surrounded the palace. Bail Organa opened the door himself as they approached.

Ferus gave a slight bow.

"We come as designates of the Emperor," he said.

"You may enter."

Bail turned and walked stiffly back into his home. Every muscle in his body told them how little he thought of them and how quickly he wanted them gone.

Ferus glanced at Hydra, but as usual couldn't tell what she was thinking. She walked swiftly, her hands concealed in her robes.

Bail led them to what must have been the palace's most formal room, used for ceremonial affairs. It was paneled with wood and topped by a domed ceiling. Inside, two women waited. Ferus recognized Breha, tall and beautiful in her white gown of plain cloth. The other woman resembled her, but was taller, with a round, pretty face and coils of dark hair around her ears.

"My wife Breha, Queen of Alderaan, and my sister-in-law, Deara, advisor to the Queen," Bail said shortly.

There was no furniture in the room, and they stood directly in the center just underneath a massive lighting fixture in the shape of a sun.

"What has brought you to Alderaan?" Bail asked.

"It is the charge of the Imperial Inquisitors to promote stability in the galaxy." Ferus trotted out the words he had been told to say before any request for information. He forged on despite the contempt evident in Bail's expression. "In order to do this, the cooperation of Senators and rulers is expected. A report has been filed by one of your citizens —"

"One of our citizens, you say," Breha said. "I don't think so. Alderaan citizens do not spy on each other."

Ferus wasn't about to debate this. Breha was most likely right. But it infuriated Ferus that his level of security clearance did not extend to the names of Imperial operatives, even code names. He didn't know who, exactly, had turned in the report of the unusual toddler.

"A report has been filed," he repeated courteously, "that makes it necessary for us to pursue an investigation onsite. We would like your permission to search the official records of Alderaan, including security reports, domestic surveillance —"

"The royal court does not spy on its citizens!" Bail's voice whipped out and echoed in the chamber.

"We leave that to you," Deara added.

"— and any and all recorded communications and citizen registries," Ferus finished. He kept his tone polite and respectful, but it did nothing to lessen Bail's obvious rage.

They all knew the outcome. Bail and Breha would give permission because they had to. They knew very well that even asking for permission was just a symbolic gesture. The Emperor had given himself the power to open any planetary records that he wished. Ferus was sure that one day soon, even this meaningless exchange wouldn't be necessary. For the present, the Emperor was still concerned with appearances.

Bail's eyes burned through him. "You don't need our permission," he said, spitting out the words. "So why put us through the hypocrisy of asking for it? Do what you will. We have nothing to hide."

As one, Bail, Breha, and Deara turned their backs on the Inquisitors and walked out.

CHAPTER THREE

As Ferus and Hydra climbed back into the airspeeder, Ferus said, "I think we should try the office of Official Records first."

"You were deferential to Bail Organa," Hydra replied, surprising him. "Why?"

"He's a Senator."

"He is the main opposition to the Emperor in the Senate. He works to destroy the Empire."

"It's easier if you avoid confrontation when you're digging on someone else's ground."

"That is a curious statement," Hydra said. "Alderaan belongs to the Empire. This is *our* ground."

Oops, Ferus thought. He had to be more careful. "I'm speaking of perception," he said. "If we push the Senator too hard, he may close access to us in ways we aren't even aware of. We don't have a lock on this planet . . . yet."

She didn't reply, and Ferus guided the airspeeder toward a cluster of official buildings in a central area of the city of Aldera. He'd have to dump Hydra somehow. She was too watchful. His job here was to investigate the report as fast as possible and then close the book on it. He didn't want her around. Obi-Wan seemed less interested in the possible presence of a Force-sensitive child than he was in getting the Inquisitors off the scent. If Ferus found the child, he'd be honor-bound to make sure he or she was protected. It could be tricky.

He was anxious to get free of Hydra and contact Amie Antin. She was a doctor and scientist, and he needed her expertise. Just days ago he'd broken into EmPal SuRecon and was able to steal some supply records. The Emperor's private medical facility had to have been the place where Darth Vader's suit had been constructed and fitted. No other place in the galaxy had that expertise. Ferus hoped that after Amie Antin analyzed the records, she'd be able to give him a clue to Vader's identity, or at least a place to start.

If his suspicions were correct, Darth Vader was a fallen Jedi. Not only that, Ferus had the nagging feeling that he'd known him. Perhaps even known him well.

If Ferus could discover the nature of Vader's injuries, he might discover who he'd been. That might give him an edge in a battle.

Because they were heading for a fight.

Vader had killed his partner Roan Lands in cold blood. He had done it just to infuriate Ferus. He had taken a life just for his own amusement.

He had to pay for that.

Ferus knew that by giving in to his rage he was jeopardizing his rediscovered grasp of the Force. He had never become a Jedi officially; he had resigned from the Order when he was still an apprentice. He knew his limitations. He wouldn't be much of a match for Vader as he was.

He had learned detachment as a Jedi Padawan, but he didn't feel detached. Not at all. A calm, steady fury was at the core of him now. It needed only a trigger to explode. He had been taught all his life that avenging a death was wrong. But this didn't feel wrong.

The Emperor had told him that he could teach Ferus about the dark side of the Force. He had told him that his anger would only make him stronger. Ferus had to admit he'd been right. You couldn't argue with results. The few times he'd tapped into his anger and felt the dark side of the Force, he'd been able to move objects at shocking velocities just by concentrating his rage.

Before he'd left Coruscant, he'd met briefly with the Emperor. Palpatine had given him a Sith Holocron, small enough to tuck into his tunic pocket. He'd told him that if he had the courage to access it he could gain great power.

He didn't tell him what he'd see. He didn't tell him what he'd learn. But the way he'd rasped the word *power,* the way he'd caressed the Holocron, had told Ferus everything. If he wanted to beat Vader, this was the only way.

He hadn't yet accessed the Holocron. He could feel it in his tunic, lending a weight out of proportion to its size. Sometimes it seemed to have warmth. Sometimes it was like an icy burn that penetrated the fabric of his clothes. Sometimes it seemed to affect him in odd ways. It felt as though the world was fracturing along invisible fault lines. There was a curious doubleness to his vision, as though he could see through things into their core underneath. Sometimes he felt a flash of contempt toward his fellow beings and their weakness.

Keeping it close felt dangerous enough.

CHAPTER FOUR

Trever Flume waved his hand over the sensor that turned the stairs into a ramp and slid down to the front door. He plugged in the exit code of Dex's hideout on Coruscant and headed out into Thugger's Alley. There was a meeting in progress, and though the topic was exciting — at last, the meeting of resistance leaders from planets all over the galaxy would take place — the talk was dull.

How could they organize a galactic resistance if they couldn't agree on the simplest thing: a place to meet?

Wil, the head of the already-legendary Eleven on Bellassa, had suggested a planet in the Outer Rim. But none of the resistance leaders thought that was a good idea. Too many checkpoints between here and there, although they would feel relatively safe once they arrived. Dex had suggested Coruscant, where he could provide security, but that suggestion was met with outrage. Put themselves right under the Emperor's nose? A good portion of the resistance leaders, the ones appearing in hologram form, had offered their homeworlds. They thought their networks were tight enough to guarantee safety, but only on their own planets. In other words, they didn't trust anyone else to provide security for them. Because they didn't yet trust each other.

Whatever. All Trever knew was that the arguments bored him silly. It was almost as bad as sitting in the Senate galleries.

Trever exited from Thugger's Alley, knowing every step he had taken down the twisting byway had been monitored by Dex's security system. He walked through the seedy levels of the Orange District, used to them now. He hardly gave a look to the other denizens of the district, where even Imperial security forces hesitated to enter. If you lived here, you knew not to initiate eye contact.

No turbolifts or pedestrian transports worked here. If a project was begun to improve the lighting, or resurface the walkways, it would be sabotaged or mysteriously destroyed, no matter how much security was used to cordon it off. So getting out of the Orange District took some time. But time was something that Trever had plenty of. That group would keep blabbing forever. No one would even notice that he'd skipped out.

Trever was wanted on his homeworld of Bellassa, but

here on Coruscant he felt oddly safer than anywhere else. He'd rather have a crush of beings to hide in. If he felt the need for air and light, he found his way to the surface and entered into the swiftly flowing currents of pedestrians in the Senate district. He felt invisible there.

And besides, before Ferus had left Coruscant, he'd given Trever a secret mission to do.

The crowds surged around him on the pedestrian walkway in the Senate district. Bright sunlight caused random flares to burst from the metallic detailing on the airspeeders flashing in the space lanes. Trever kept his eyes open for Imperial security, which sometimes initiated random ID checks.

He was often alone now. Astri's son, Lune Oddo, was on the secret asteroid base that Ferus had established. Lune had been in training with Ry-Gaul, but the silent Jedi had brought him to Garen Muln for more lessons. Even though Garen was frail now, he had a special, new-found gift for teaching. Garen had been one of the most daring Jedi pilots back when the Jedi were still around. Now he was in seclusion on the asteroid and had, he said, discovered new parts of himself, like patience.

Trever was surprised to find himself missing Lune. He'd never paid much attention to the kid until the eight-year-old had been kidnapped and forced to enroll in the new Imperial Naval Academy. Trever had enrolled in order to get him out, and he'd discovered that the little guy had full-moon smarts and nerves of durasteel. Not to mention that he was pretty good company. They'd spent a bit of time together before Ry-Gaul had whisked him off to the asteroid. Maybe it was the spooky Force-connection Lune had, but the kid definitely kept you on your toes.

Trever hopped on a moving ramp that brought him up another fifty levels in the crisscrossing levels and mid-levels of the district. As the ramp moved upward, a new perspective of the shimmering buildings appeared. His gaze rested on the ruined Jedi Temple, now directly in front of him.

He turned his head. He'd been inside the Temple with Ferus, early in their friendship. He'd hung onto that spire and followed Ferus inside. Even he, with no Force connection at all, had felt the power that still hummed inside those walls.

It hurt his eyes to see it now.

He'd heard the ruined Temple was now a site of ghoulish fascination to the elite of Coruscant. It was a place where so many Jedi had died. It was considered a mark of status if you'd been permitted to tour it. The whole idea disgusted him. He wouldn't tell Ferus. He knew how much it would upset him.

Just then, to his surprise, he caught sight of Flame above, moving through the crowds. As the ramp moved upward, he saw her turn onto another walkway. He leaped off the ramp and followed her.

He caught up with her near the fountains on the edge of one of the many plazas surrounding the Senate building.

"Sightseeing?" he asked as he came up beside her.

She must have jumped a meter. "I didn't see you," she said. "Trever, you gave me a fright. I'm always on the lookout for an Imperial ID check."

"Sorry." He leaned back against the fountain wall, feeling the spray against his neck. "What are you doing in these parts?"

"Is the meeting over?" she asked, running over his words. An anxious look was on her face. "They asked me to leave so they could debate more freely."

"They're still blabbing away." Trever shook his head. "You'd think a bunch of resistance fighters would have more nerve. Everyone's afraid of being caught."

"It's a question of trust," Flame said, looking at the play of sunlight on the fountain. Her green eyes narrowed. "Decisions like this take a cohesiveness that the group doesn't have yet."

"Cohesiveness?" Trever snorted. "It takes guts. That's all."

"They've already proved their courage," Flame chided gently. She frowned. "But I don't like this. I'm afraid Moonstrike will fall apart. I had a meeting with Bail Organa. I was given an introduction to him by one of the resistance leaders, a former trusted associate of his. I asked him to join Moonstrike, and he refused. He said there was no resistance on Alderaan and that he was committed to working through the Senate. He must be lying," she said, clasping her hands together. "There's got to be an underground movement on that planet. What does Ferus say?"

"He only just got there. He didn't say much."

"Bail Organa is the key," Flame said. "If only we had Senators in Moonstrike! That would lend it legitimacy. We could form a galaxy-wide movement for certain then, with a political arm and a military one. But if Bail Organa refuses, others will." She turned to Trever. "Do you think Ferus could convince him?"

"Ferus is undercover," Trever said. "Organa thinks he's part of the Empire, remember?"

"Well, he'd have to reveal his identity as a double agent, of course," Flame said. "But Bail Organa is trustworthy. We need him, Trever!"

"I'll ask Ferus," Trever said. He'd do just about anything for Flame. Rumor had it she'd sacrificed a pretty sweet life and a personal fortune to start the Moonstrike movement. Next to Ferus, he admired her more than anyone in the galaxy. "But all I can do is ask. You can't make Ferus do something he doesn't think is right. He's really annoying that way."

"Tell him how important it is," Flame urged.

Trever nodded, noting how strained Flame seemed.

She was usually so cool and collected, even under blaster-fire. He guessed it was because she was so close to her goal.

"I'm counting on you," Flame said. She smiled and reached out to tug at the brim of the cap he wore to conceal his bluish hair. "As I always do."

The affection of the gesture pleased him as much as the confidence in her eyes. "I won't let you down," he promised.

He continued on his way. He looked above and saw the tall Republica 500 tower ahead. Ferus had contacted him earlier that day and asked him to check out the security measures there.

Ferus still felt bad that when he'd broken into EmPal SuRecon he'd had to leave one of the scientists, Linna Naltree, behind. She'd willingly returned to continue as the barbaric scientist Jenna Zan Arbor's assistant, in order to ensure that Lune and Ferus would be able to escape. Ferus owed her a debt, and he intended to get her out if he could. The first step was to see if she was staying at the Republica tower along with Zan Arbor, who had demanded an apartment in that most exclusive housing tower in the city.

They still didn't know what Zan Arbor was working on, but they knew it involved Darth Vader. More investigation was needed. Linna might know by now what the secret project was. If they could get to her, they could discover what she knew and free her from Zan Arbor's grip. A little surveillance was the first step.

Trever stopped in an exclusive florist that he knew sold exotic blooms from all over the galaxy. He balked at the prices and finally chose the cheapest thing he could find, a small plant with vibrant yellow leaves native to the planet Huro. He asked them to wrap it extra carefully, with plenty of their signature lilac gemweb fabric and trailing rainbow ribbons. He got attitude from the clerk but he didn't care. He picked it up and headed for the plaza in front of the tower.

The elite of Coruscant swirled through the plaza, some striding forward quickly, as though they were on their way to a crucial appointment, others carefully balancing ridiculous coiffures and headdresses, walking in a slow, stately fashion so that others would notice them. Trever felt invisible as he moved through the crowd. No one noticed just another insignificant boy, one of the hundreds who ran errands and did the Senators' bidding. They were on the lowest rung of the Senate hierarchy. Trever had been sure to get hold of the brown caps they wore pulled down to their eyebrows. Under the brim, his gaze could study the front of the tower and see through the massive transparisteel doors into the lobby. Within only a few moments he'd scoped out the security.

Not completely, of course. He knew from being a street thief on Bellassa that there was security you saw and security you could only guess at. He would be able to make it into the lobby without trouble, thanks to his package. But he'd have to do some curvy tricks to get himself inside a turbolift.

Luckily, when it came to curvy tricks, he was an expert.

Ferus had only asked him to scope out the obvious and speculate on the rest. Ferus hadn't asked him to actually break into Zan Arbor's apartment.

But he was going to anyway.

CHAPTER FIVE

Ferus left the airspeeder with Hydra and took off his Inquisitor robe, stuffing it in his pack. He immediately felt better, lighter, and easier in his mind.

He struck out into the streets of Aldera. Like a Jedi on a mission, he wanted his boots on the ground. Sometimes a simple walk through a city plaza could tell you more about the state of a planet than a full briefing.

Aldera was built on an island over a vast shallow lake. Most of the buildings were built from the same glowing white stone, with domes and towers thrusting up into a sky that seemed to arc like a delicate teacup overhead. The people of Aldera went about their business with pleasant expressions, hailing friends, slowing their steps to admire the day, stopping at a café. Unlike the other worlds he had visited, Alderaan didn't seem touched by the hand of the Empire.

And that worried him.

He didn't know if the Emperor had plans for Alderaan, but he sensed that the people here thought he would never dare to. They were protected by their Queen, by their Senator, and by their own peacefulness. Alderaan had banned weapons long ago, and its citizens had found a way to coexist without the strife and anger that split other societies.

Ferus knew that sooner or later Palpatine would turn his eye on Alderaan. Bail was too powerful a figure to allow to remain so influential. It might take months or years, but it would happen.

Ferus felt his comlink signal buzz against his side. He saw that it was a coded message. Hoping it was Amie Antin, he drifted over to a small park tucked in between two buildings. The park was in shade and no one was sitting there. He stood and answered.

"I'm glad I could reach you. It's Amie."

"You have news for me?"

"I've gone over the information you forwarded to me from the break-in at EmPal. I haven't found much. Except . . . during the time period you gave me there was an emergency shipment of a special strain of bacta that has been proven effective in cases of severe burns and regeneration of tissue. That would be standard equipment for any med center. Except . . ."

Amie's voice faded out, and he couldn't tell if it was the transmission or her hesitancy. "Except?" he prompted.

"Added to this emergency shipment was a trio of detoxification drugs and devices specifically designed to treat a being with heavy metal contamination. Which means that most likely a patient had been injured in either a mine explosion or, more likely, a volcanic eruption in which the lava held an unusually high concentration of metal allotropes . . . ."

"Amie, I beg you. Get to the point."

"So I researched mining planets and volcanic planets, but the database was just too large to pin down. So I went back to the supply list and found something I'd overlooked. Well, I hadn't overlooked it, but it hadn't seemed significant. One of the med agents ordered for the center had been ordered in a very small quantity, too little, really, to be logical if it was a standard order for outfitting a new care facility. This was a rush shipment of a very expensive medication, which only has one medical use: to neutralize an extremely rare but toxic heavy metal that is only found on two hundred and eleven planets . . ." Amie took a breath ". . . which I cross-checked for volcanic activity. The weird thing is that this allotrope can't survive in normal lava; the lava has to be a bit cooler. Say about eight hundred degrees."

"That sounds pretty hot to me."

"That's because you're not a volcano. So this particular allotrope stays liquid, which increases its toxicity. So then I cross-checked for volcanic eruptions in the last year of the Clone Wars, and amazingly enough, because this never happens, only forty-three planets met all the criteria."

Ferus sighed. Forty-three wasn't bad, but it wasn't close enough. It would take time to narrow down the list. "Thank you, Amie, you can send the —"

"Wait. I'm not finished. I took the list to Dex, and Oryon was there. Remember he was a master spy at the end of the Clone Wars? Well, he recognized one of the planets. Reports at the end of the Clone Wars cited it as a hideout for the Separatist Council. Mustafar. Look, I'm a scientist, so I don't like jumping to conclusions. All of this is speculative. But if I *had* to guess where this patient had been injured, I would bet on Mustafar."

"Mustafar. I've never heard of it."

"That's not surprising. Nobody in their right mind would go there. It's a remote planet in the Outer Rim. It has a gas-giant twin, Jestefad. It has unspeakable heat, rivers of boiling lava, and the volcanoes are in a continual phase of eruption. Your basic nightmare planet."

A perfect place for a Sith to be born, Ferus thought.

But what could he do with the information? He could hardly go tearing off to the Outer Rim. There was no telling if he'd find anything there, anyway. In his bones, he felt whatever information he needed to defeat Darth Vader lay here in the Core, in the everyday activities of the new Empire. In his own intuition.

In the Holocron.

That voice . . . what was it? Not his own. It had

sprang up in his mind, and the Holocron seemed to burn his chest in response. Ferus put his hand over it.

"There's one other thing," Amie said. "The Moonstrike meeting isn't going well."

Ferus felt a surge of annoyance. *Why was she bothering him with trivialities? Amie was foolish and naïve.*

That voice again . . . it wasn't his.

No, Amie was brave and resourceful. She'd been a doctor on her homeworld on Bellassa. She'd kept out of the Eleven as long as she could, but only so she could continue her work. She had a son back on Bellassa whom she pined for.

That makes her a weak link in the chain.

No. He would never consider Amie weak, or capable of betrayal.

Everyone is capable of betrayal. Everyone has a weak point.

Ferus dropped his hand from the Holocron. It felt as though it had burned him. The voice in his head was too insistent. Where did it come from?

It comes from you. It is your true voice that is speaking.

Agitated, Ferus reached out for the Force. He needed to fight the voice, and he couldn't do it alone.

He'd never had thoughts like that about Amie. They weren't true. She was a courageous, compassionate woman.

The Sith Holocron cooled against him.

He looked down at his fingers. They were reddened as if they'd been held to a flame.

"So if you could just consider it," Amie went on, "we would be grateful."

He had lost the thread of what she'd been saying. With difficulty, Ferus wrenched his attention back to her and replayed her words in his head. "The asteroid must remain a secret between all of us," he said. "If we expose it, we endanger any future Jedi I may find."

"Ferus, I respect your mission, I do," Amie said. "But so far, all we've found is that the Jedi who haven't been eradicated have gone so deeply underground that they are impossible to find. And the resistance is starting here, now. We need your help."

"I'll consider it," he said finally. "I can only promise you that."

They ended the communication. Ferus looked at his burned fingertips. He felt shaken. It was the first time he felt that the Holocron had influenced his mind.

Was this just a taste of what could happen to him, with a Sith Holocron so near?

Ferus walked all the way to the northern outskirts of the city and reached the park. It was built over the lake that surrounded the city of Aldera and mimicked the grasslands that covered much of the planet. Ferus knew that there were thousands of varieties of grasses on Alderaan, and he could see that many of them were represented here. The grasses had been planted in swaths of undulating rows, each in a different color of green and blue and gold, and the colors seemed even more intense on this day of bright sunlight.

Children ran through the grasses or congregated on the soft sandy areas that were interspersed with the grass to provide space for play and picnics. Ferus made his way to the very edge of the park. There was a gradual slope upward and then a long flight of steps made from blocks of white stone. He climbed up to the vantage point above.

He now stood on a sandstone bluff overlooking the lake, which stretched to the horizon. To his left was the main spaceport of Alderaan, a busy place with constant traffic. He could see the glint of sunlight on the cruisers that were almost constantly landing and taking off. To his right was the expanse of blue lake.

The railing had been designed to look like braided vines. He wandered along it until his gaze found what he was looking for. Despite the careful repair work, he could see where the railing was newly mended. If the woman in the report had fallen, she would have landed on the sandstone rocks below, and would have been seriously injured.

Ferus turned in a full circle to survey his surroundings. Although the smell of the grass and the water made it seem as though he was in the country, he was surrounded by the city. Here near the edge of the park the buildings appeared to be more industrial — warehouses and vertical hangars, most likely for the nearby spaceport.

Perhaps he wouldn't have noticed it if he hadn't been trained at the Temple. Perhaps it would have seemed just another flash from descending aircraft. Ferus rotated again, pretending to take in the view. Yes, that was it. The building to his right, the one closest to the park . . . someone was using electrobinoculars. He'd seen the flash of sunlight on the lenses.

Was someone spying on the park?

Ferus turned and began to walk at a leisurely pace back down the wide stairs, and then through the ornamental grass. Suddenly a toddler darted in front of him. Ferus stepped back.

"Sorry." A woman with warm eyes and a ready smile scooped up the toddler. "Tula, you've got to watch where you're going."

"I should have, as well," Ferus said. "This is a beautiful park."

"Your first time here?" She pushed her hair out of her eyes and smiled. "It's a great spot. It never gets too crowded because it's out of the way." Her toddler began to wriggle, and she gently set her down. "But tomorrow is when you should be here. The gingerbells are ready to bloom."

"I'm afraid I don't know much about flowers," Ferus said.

"You must not be from Alderaan, then."

"I'm a visitor."

She crouched and pointed to a small bud almost hidden in the grass. "There are thousands of these in the park. They're famous on Alderaan because they all bloom on the same day. The park is hosting a festival here. Everyone who knows the park will come. It's an amazing sight. They let the children pick all the blossoms." She straightened and began to run after her toddler. "You should come!" she called to Ferus over her shoulder.

Yes, he would come. It would be a perfect opportunity to observe the children.

What did Siri Tachi used to say? *"If you want to get lucky, open your eyes."* Ferus smiled, remembering his Master's brusque way of talking, her irreverence, her style. He still missed her.

Attachment — forbidden or . . . normal?

He walked along the far side of the park and crossed a wide boulevard to get close to the building he'd observed. It was some kind of warehouse, with a security system but no personnel. Ferus bypassed the standard security entry code with ease. It was a skill he'd learned in his old profession, the business he'd started with Roan. Although technically they operated on the right side of the law, it was occasionally helpful to push the line a bit.

Faced with a bank of turbolifts, he oriented himself

quickly and chose one that reached the highest floors facing west. He zoomed upward. He had counted the floors from the ground and he guessed he'd seen the flash from the two hundred and seventh floor.

Ferus walked out cautiously. He reached for the Force, letting it tell him if there was any danger. He felt no vibrations, no clues as to what lay ahead. He didn't feel a trace of the Living Force. It felt to him as though the floor was deserted.

He moved cautiously toward the door he guessed would have the window he'd seen from below. He listened carefully at the door but heard nothing.

He bypassed the security code and entered.

The room was empty. Completely empty. Nothing had been stored here for some time. He could smell the dust. So why had it been locked? He walked to the window. The dust had been disturbed. Someone had cleared a clean space to look out.

He looked down at the park. From here he could pick out the woman with the toddler who had talked to him. Now she was with a tall, thin man who picked up the toddler. The baby's father. They started to exit the park. Ferus swept the park with his gaze and the boulevard below. Everyone else seemed normal, too. No one was moving quickly or keeping underneath the underhangs. If there was anything suspicious, it wasn't evident from here.

He took out his own electrobinoculars and trained them below. From here you could see the fence clearly; he could even pick out the point of repair. If he lifted his gaze just a fraction, the spaceport was directly in his line of vision. He had a close-up view of the main landing platform for galactic traffic arrivals and departures. He could pick out cruiser models. He could see pilots, insignias, flags of other planets, supplies being offloaded from freighters.

Ferus lowered his electrobinoculars. On the day the child had showed Force-potential, perhaps there had been a lull. Or a flurry of activity that had caused the watcher's attention to divert to the park below. The watcher would have noted the toddler moving to save the caregiver and would have recorded it, perhaps just to pad a report so that a superior would be pleased. The watcher would know, as an Imperial spy, how important it was to inform on anyone or anything.

The report on the toddler was nothing compared to this. No one on Alderaan could come and go without being seen. Ferus knew that all Alderaanians were required to pass through the main spaceport before going offworld.

Ferus leaned forward. He had just noticed that the dust had been disturbed on the sill to the window, too. Luckily he hadn't smeared the impression when he'd leaned forward. He could just make out some letters and numbers, as though someone had quickly scrawled them in the dust.

LCS . . . then a smudge. Then . . . *79244-12u712*

Ferus quickly committed the letters and numbers to memory.

He just had to figure out what they meant.

CHAPTER SIX

Vader was ushered into the Emperor's office imme-diately. Sly Moore opened the door and withdrew quickly, as if to escape a blast. Not a good sign.

His Master waited by the window, staring out at the luxury craft streaming into the Senate landing platform. In the first flush of the Empire, Senators were taking advantage of the end of the tiresome regulations of the Republic. Regulations that safeguarded banking, corpo-ration greed, mining, environmental concerns . . . they had only prevented the outrageous profits that could be made by the few at the expense of the many. Now the Senators could exploit their connections to the great mining and corporate concerns and, as a result, they were richer than ever. It was one way Palaptine assured their loyalty.

"We need to discuss Operation Twilight," Palpatine snapped. "I'm tired of excuses. You promised me speed and efficiency."

Vader would have to be careful.

"We are very close," Vader said. "Less than a week. The first step of the final phase is in only a few days."

"You must go to Alderaan," Palpatine said.

It was never a good idea to allow surprise to show. "Yes, Master." He kept his silence, awaiting his orders.

"Senator Organa is our enemy. Behind my back he is trying to rally a group of Senators to fight against the installation of Imperial Governors."

"They will fail."

"Of course," Palpatine rasped. "I *control* the Senate. But its voice will be heard. Organa is a problem. We must move up our plan. We must involve him in Twilight."

"We have tried," Vader said.

"I am tired of *failure!*"

"Yes, Master."

Palpatine tucked his hands inside the wide sleeves of his robe and strolled to a different window. "Ferus Olin is on Alderaan," he remarked. "Working on some-thing . . . unimportant. Chasing Force-sensitives. He can do no harm. But your paths will cross on Alderaan, no doubt."

"I do not know why you continue to promote Olin," Vader said. "You *know* where his loyalties lie."

His Master turned to face him. A grimace of amuse-ment was on his face. "Loyalties change. Surely you are proof of that."

"He will defect to the Empire?"

Palpatine turned away again. "He will do as I *foresee*. He wants power and control. He is *strong* in the Force. A decision awaits him."

It was a riddle, yes, but its meaning was clear. Vader's suspicions were correct. With his ruined body he was a disappointment. His Master would promote Ferus until Ferus defected or until Vader destroyed him.

The confrontation lay ahead. He had already set the trap by killing Roan Lands. When Ferus came at him, it would be with rage, not control.

He will not know how to use his anger, Vader thought. *It will be so easy.*

Easy things were not satisfying for him. They never had been.

This would be the exception.

CHAPTER SEVEN

Chin resting on her hands, Astri Oddo used her fingers to prop open her eyes. She'd been staring at data for six hours straight. It was four o'clock in the morning, and everything was starting to blur.

"Want some more of this?" Clive Flax waved a triple-strength protein stimulant drink in the air.

Astri let her head fall on the desk with a soft thud. "I need sleep."

"Wimp."

Astri rolled her head to look at Clive. "There's nothing here. We've gone through every record we have. You think Flame is a code name for Eve Yarrow. We've looked through every file on Yarrow, and there's nothing linking her to Flame."

"Isn't that strange?" Clive said. He began to manipulate the special repulsorlift chair Dex used when he had to move fast. "We know she's not dead. We know she left her homeworld of Acherin." He spun the chair around to face Astri. "Isn't it weird that she just . . . disappeared?"

"No," Astri said tiredly. "It's not weird, Clive. It's normal. I mean, it's the new version of normal. She was imprisoned by the Empire. Eve Yarrow had every reason to disappear. She managed to get all her wealth off-planet, and she most likely bought herself a new identity."

"That's another piece that doesn't fit," Clive insisted, making lazy circles in the air on the chair. "How did she manage to smuggle all of her wealth out of a planet occupied by the Empire — *after* she'd been arrested?"

"Maybe she'd prepared ahead of time. Most rich people have a backup plan. Maybe she was just smart." Astri shrugged. Even the small movement made her feel tired.

"Or connected."

"Face it, Clive." Astri closed the holofile on Dex's desk. "We're done. There are no records left to search. Nothing more I can slice into. We've gone as far as we can go."

Clive leaped out of the repulsorlift chair as it was still spinning. "You're right!" He hurried to the door.

"Where are you going?"

"To wake up Keets!"

Astri rested her cheeks on her hands and sighed. Time was running out. The group was having trouble settling on the first Moonstrike meeting, but they would find a way. Flame was a hero to them all. It was only Clive who felt something was off. If he was right — and Astri doubted that he was — every resistance movement in the galaxy could be compromised.

Who was Flame? A great hero . . . or an agent of the Empire?

Hero . . . agent.

Hero . . . agent . . .

"Wake up, my beauty!" Clive's voice caused her to jerk and bang her chin on the table. She'd fallen into a doze. "We've got work to do!"

Keets looked as sleepy as she did. "What's going on?"

Clive guided him to a chair at Dex's long dataport desk and pushed him into it.

"We're investigating Flame. We haven't told anyone because, well, at this point, we're a little short on facts."

"Meaning we don't have any," Astri said.

"Meaning we're basically going on my intuition," Clive explained, "which has never failed me in the past."

Astri raised an eyebrow.

"Well, okay, it's failed me a number of times, but never mind. Didn't you tell me that before you went underground you'd done a major exposé of the Banking Clan?"

Keets nodded. "My editor wouldn't publish it.

Somebody leaned on him. So I quit. Then the Empire put a death mark on my head. Not a good day."

"What did you uncover that would scare the Empire so much?"

"Well, it was before the Clone Wars were over," Keets said. "The Chancellor still needed the support of the Senate. They weren't exactly licking the hem of his robes back then. Not like now." He yawned. "So I dug up the fact that Palpatine had helped the Banking Clan develop a whole system of secret bank accounts for huge corporations on a ring of planets. They weren't subject to any accounting or taxes. That way Palpatine had the support of the clan, as well as the richest corporations in the galaxy. Of course, this isn't much of a surprise now. Back then, it could have made a difference. He was costing planets billions of credits in lost revenue."

"Do you think those accounts still exist?" Clive asked.

"Of course they do," Keets said, rubbing his eyes. "The only difference is that now Palpatine himself controls them. Credits keep pouring into them, and he doesn't take anything, but he knows it's there if he needs it. It's a brilliant backup plan."

"So, if a wealthy person wanted to hide wealth, it would be a perfect system for them."

"Sure." Keets looked more awake now. "What are

you getting at? You're going to have to bring me up to hyperspeed."

"You're saying that Flame's wealth — the credits she keeps spreading around — that it's actually held in *Empire-controlled accounts?*" Astri looked at Clive, astounded.

"I don't know," Clive said. "But wouldn't it be a good idea to find out? Look, if she's Eve Yarrow, that means she left Acherin with a vast fortune. She couldn't just walk into any bank in the galaxy and deposit it without someone reporting on it."

"There are plenty of places in the galaxy to hide wealth," Astri observed.

"Sure, for criminals," Clive said. "But what about upstanding citizens? How could they do it without the Empire's help? It's a whole new galaxy now, my beauty. The Empire's eye is everywhere."

Astri shook her head. "You're jumping to conclusions again."

"So we jump! We don't have time to stay put," Clive declared. He turned to Keets. "Do you still have your notes?"

"Sure. I loaded everything onto Dex's databank. He's trying to collect all the information he can so that any resistance will have a data library to go to once we start really organizing," Keets said.

"Can you trace a specific corporation's holdings? Astri wasn't able to. It's buried."

"No, it *disappeared*," Astri said sharply. "If it was just buried, I would have found it."

"I'm sure the Empire wiped it. But I have the records from before the Clone Wars officially ended," Keets said. "I might be able to turn something up. Yarrow Industries, right?" He moved to the dataport. His fingers flipped through holofiles while he searched. Clive drummed his fingers on the desk.

"Here we go. The operations for Yarrow Industries were moved near the end of the war to Niro 11. That's a moon ringing the planet Niro, which was once pretty much owned by the Banking Clan."

Astri leaned forward. "Does it say who authorized the transfer?"

"No, just that it was authorized. Some top-level Imperial, I'm sure."

Astri read over Keet's shoulder. "Wait a second. That's standard bank security coding. I might be able to slice into the records." Keets moved over, and she sat at the computer. Her fingers flew as she concentrated, wide awake now. In a few minutes, she let out a low whistle. "I can't break in, but I can see that the account is active. There's levels of privacy code here. A trigger if it gets accessed from the outside. It'll send off an alert."

"So what do you think?" Clive asked.

Astri spun around on her chair. "I think we're going to Niro 11."

CHAPTER EIGHT

The sight of thousands of blooming yellow flowers amid the grass was amazing indeed. As the park came into view, Ferus stopped walking just to take it in. It was like a blue, green, and golden sea that undulated in waves caused by the breeze, each shiver uncovering another vivid shade.

"What's the matter?" Hydra asked next to him.

"The flowers," Ferus said, still visually stunned.

"Oh. That." She kept up her pace, not pausing a bit. "I'll start interviewing the parents."

He had tried to get rid of her, but could think of no plausible excuse to keep Hydra away. She had researched the park and knew about the festival, and of course the two of them could cover more ground than one Inquisitor could.

The park was full of children, as though the city of Aldera had shaken out all their youngsters into this one area. Children running, children squealing, children gathering baskets of the bell-shaped flowers. As they walked into the park, one of them, a charming girl with golden curls, threw a handful of flowers into the air as if in greeting. Golden blossoms fell on Hydra's brown hood. The disgust on Hydra's face would have been comical if the whole thing weren't so serious.

"It will be hard to keep track of all these children," Ferus said.

"That's our job," Hydra said.

Ferus could only bear Hydra's company for so long. "Let's split up so we can cover more territory," he suggested. She glided away.

Ferus called on the Force to help him slow time and sharpen his perceptions. It was a state of alertness that was very close to battle-mind. Now instead of an indistinguishable mass of happy faces he picked out individual after individual. The greedy boy who could not stop chewing his muffins as he gathered more flowers, the little girl sitting with a small hill of flowers in her lap, the minder who was weaving the flowers into a wreath for her silent and watchful charge.

A little girl caught his attention, a glint of sun on hair so pale it was the color of moonbeams. She scooped up handfuls of petals and scattered them as she ran. A smaller girl followed her, mimicking her movements. Although only a toddler — she couldn't have been walking for very long — she ran in wide loops through the long grass, without the usual unsteadiness of a girl her age. As Ferus watched, a toy, a model of a starfighter, winged through the air toward the girl. She caught it in her hand and sent it shooting back, looping in the same way she was running. As she ran she caught the toy again and flung it backhanded this time, where it looped and came toward her again.

Not easy. Extraordinary balance and reflexes for someone that young. An observer would merely think her . . . precocious.

He strolled forward, keeping a parallel track. As he got closer he gathered in the Force around him and searched, but could feel no answering Force from the little girl. If she had a Force connection, he couldn't feel it. But nevertheless he felt . . . something. Instinct pricked the back of his neck.

They were approaching the stairway to the top of the bluff. The girl ran up it, following the taller, pale-haired girl. Ferus followed.

"Winter!" the toddler called out the name, and the pale-haired girl turned. The toddler pointed straight ahead at the gate.

"They fixed it," the older girl said.

A slender young woman with coiled braids hurried up the steps past Ferus. "There you are, you two!"

Ferus tuned out the noise of children's laughter, the wind in the tall grasses. He needed to hear this conversation.

The young woman put her hand on the toddler's hair

and stroked it gently. "Yes, Leia. I see it, too. No one will get hurt again."

"Memily won't fall."

"No, blossom. I won't fall." The young woman hugged the little girl.

Leia?

Was that a common name on Alderaan? Could the toddler be Bail's daughter? Ferus searched his memory. He'd read the file on the palace inhabitants on the way to Alderaan. Winter was Leia's playmate, who lived in the royal household.

Stunned, Ferus walked away from the group before they noticed him. So Leia was the toddler who had saved her caregiver. Leia had a possible Force connection. Leia was the child the Inquisitors were looking for.

Did Bail know?

A new thought blazed across Ferus's brain.

Did *Obi-Wan* know?

Why else had he been so insistent that Ferus travel to Alderaan?

Well, thanks, Obi-Wan. Maybe the next time you send me off to investigate, you'll give me all the facts.

Ferus tried to shake off his annoyance. This went beyond his own feelings. There was an Imperial spy on Alderaan, and Bail's family was in danger.

Hydra moved toward him, her cloak sweeping the ground behind her. Ferus noted how she moved straight through the grass, not caring about the children, her face impassive, never smiling. The mothers and fathers at the park had noticed her, and Ferus saw how they drew closer to their children as Hydra walked by.

He signaled her not to approach him and headed for the exit. It was important that he not be seen with her.

At the exit to the park, she came up to him. "Find anything?"

He looked at her, into her dark eyes, shiny and impersonal as stones. He would have to protect Bail's family against her, too.

"No," he said. "Nothing."

CHAPTER NINE

Later that day, Ferus left Hydra at the office of Official Records. Reluctantly he made his way back to the palace. He had no idea what he would do. He couldn't just come out and tell Bail he feared for his family. Bail would think it was a trick.

He made his way through the official entrance, down the twisting path. He struck off in a different direction this time. The flowers gave way to fruit trees, then vegetables in neat rows. He was in the kitchen garden now.

Double doors were flung open onto a small slate patio, and he heard the sound of humming and smelled fresh bread. Ferus walked forward.

The same young woman he'd seen in the park — Memily — was now wearing a long apron and a colorful headwrap. She stood at the counter, chopping fruit. Around her was a spotless kitchen, a long wooden table that stretched the length of the room, mellow wood polished from years of use. A counter held six loaves of warm bread.

"Stop right there," the young woman said without turning. "Whoever it is, you should know better than to invade my kitchen on baking day."

"Then you shouldn't let the smell out into the garden."

She turned, smiling, wiping her hands on her apron. "You must be here for the meeting. You can go through those doors and turn left for the reception rooms. Here."

She cut a thick slice of bread and spread it with a honey mixture. "I'll be bringing refreshments to the meeting, but you can sneak a piece. One slice, that's all."

Ferus took a bite of the bread and let out a sigh. "Best in the galaxy," he praised.

"I don't fall for flattery."

"I didn't think you would."

He munched on the bread, watching Memily's quick, efficient movements as she chopped fruit and then spooned it into small pastry shells.

"For the children," she said. "They call these Memily's baskets." She smiled. "I've seen Senator Organa sneak them, too."

"I don't blame him," Ferus said. "The family seems very close," he added.

"Oh, yes, it's a pleasure to work here. The children fill the house with laughter. I do double duty, you know, and watch them sometimes just for the fun of it. This is a royal household, but you'd never know it. There's no protocol here. The Queen has been here in the kitchen, kneading bread with me, many times. Leia, too. They want to bring her up right, you know. Strong and sure, but knowing that she's blessed to have so much. You have to start early. When she came to them, it was a stroke of good fortune. We knew how sad the Queen had been."

Ferus nodded, but he wasn't sure what Memily meant. "It must have been hard, to see her that way," he said. Sometimes a neutral comment would bring you information you wouldn't get with a question.

"She wanted her own children. It wasn't meant to be. But a newborn comes and it becomes the child you're meant to have. Leia has been a great gift to the household."

Leia was adopted. The news surprised Ferus. And Leia had been a newborn when she came here, which meant she'd been adopted at the end of the Clone Wars. That made sense. The war had created many orphans.

Ferus stood. "Thank you for the bread."

Memily smiled her good-bye and he left the kitchen.

Ferus headed toward the public wing of the house, where Bail had received him earlier. He found himself in a broad hallway and heard the murmur of voices. He drew closer, trying to focus on the sounds. Normally they would be undetectable, but he reached out with the Force.

". . . I declined because I think it's too soon," Bail said. "Breha agrees with me."

"I see your thinking. Alderaan can always join a united resistance movement once it's firmly established. There's no need to place us in danger."

"That's not my reason, Deara." Breha spoke now. "We would share the risk if we felt the moment was right. That's not the issue. If you disagree, please tell us. We value your opinion."

"I agree with you and Bail, Breha. But there is something else. Something disturbing I've heard. There are many in Aldera who feel they should form a resistance movement. And prepare for invasion, should that come. They feel we should reexamine our weapons policy in light of what's happening on other planets. What if Alderaan is invaded?"

"If Alderaan is invaded we can hardly hope to defeat the Empire's forces," Bail said. "We have no weapons, no attack ships."

"But the people feel they would want to defend themselves."

"If we got through the Clone Wars without arming ourselves, we can outlast the Empire," Breha said, her tone sharp.

"Of course. I'm just repeating what I've heard."

Ferus heard the sound of boots hurrying along the hallway. He faded back and concealed himself around a corner.

"Raymus Antilles!" It was the Queen's voice. "We started the meeting without you, but we can —"

"I have news."

The doors shut behind Raymus. Suddenly Ferus couldn't hear a thing. He walked closer, making no sound. His breathing slowed; his movements were quick but completely noiseless. Not a rustle of cloth, not a brush against a wall, not even a disturbance of air. Ferus closed his eyes. He let the Force guide him. The noises of the palace came to him, sounds he hadn't even registered, sounds he hadn't heard. Conversation outside in the garden. Memily closing the oven door. An insect was scratching behind a wall. . . .

The door was wood, and there was a new barrier behind it . . . something to muffle sound. Durasteel most likely. But even durasteel was slightly porous. It was made up of particles, like anything else, like fabric, like wood. And through those spaces he could slip, all attention, everything focused on sound.

Raymus: He has landed at the spaceport. He'll be here in moments.

Bail: This is not unexpected. Palpatine was bound to send his enforcer sooner or later. The question is, what does he want?

Queen Breha: What should we do?

Raymus: You must receive him, of course. But Bail, if you have a message for Mon Mothma, give it to me now. I can still slip away and get to the Tantive. *If he is authorized by the Emperor to search he won't find anything.*

Bail: Here. Take this.

Raymus: They could shut down our landing platform, our hangars . . . they could imprison Bail. . . .

Breha: He wouldn't dare.

Raymus: They've done it to others.

Breha: We must give the appearance of cooperation. We must avoid an Imperial Governor at all costs.

Bail: Go now. Do not travel to Coruscant directly but head out to the TerraAsta spaceport and get lost in the heavy galactic traffic there.

Suddenly, Ferus felt the dark side of the Force surge. It was a feeling he was accustomed to now. Usually it was followed by the swish of a cape and the *whoosh, whoosh* of a breath mask. Darth Vader had arrived.

Following his Force connection now, Ferus headed down through the sunny hallways to the back of the palace. He saw Vader immediately. The Dark Lord strode directly through the vegetable garden, crushing everything beneath his boots.

It was time to stall him. Ferus needed to give Raymus a chance to get away.

He found a floor-to-ceiling window that slid open noiselessly with a wave of his hand over the sensor. Vader looked over as he stepped out onto a stone terrace.

"Lord Vader," Ferus said, crossing to greet him. He looked down pointedly at the plants, twisted and matted, at Vader's feet. "Doing your usual work, I see."

"Why are you here?" Vader demanded.

"I needed permission from Senator Organa to search classified files," he said.

"You hardly need *permission*," Vader said.

Behind Vader, he suddenly saw a flash of white, a blur of pink. Winter and Leia ran through a fountain at the far end of the garden.

His heartbeat accelerated, but he knew Vader would be able to detect any nerves, so he used his Force-training to slow it down. He would need to distract him, though. If indeed Leia had a Force-connection, Vader might be able to pick it up.

"The investigation is going well," he said. "Inquisitor Hydra is at the office of Official Records right now."

Vader made an impatient gesture.

"But I'm sure we'll conclude this investigation soon," Ferus continued. "Our next stop is Mustafar," he added.

Vader didn't move. He didn't betray surprise, but Ferus felt it. For the first time, he had penetrated Vader's mask. He knew it. He had rocked him. If they'd been dueling, this would have counted as the first contact, the first aggressive move that would surprise his opponent.

Behind Vader, he saw Breha quickly hustle the girls out of the garden.

"This is a waste of my time," Vader said. "As usual."

He pushed by Ferus.

Ferus wasn't insulted. Not in the least.

Mustafar. Amie had been right. Whatever had happened to Vader had happened there.

Now he just had to find out what.

CHAPTER TEN

Mustafar!

What did Olin mean? What did he know?

Vader could feel his heartbeat push the breath through his mask more quickly. Little explosions of air rang in his ears. How he wished he could throw off this mask, peel off this armor, and get the body he knew back! The strong legs and arms, the fluid movements, the ability to throw himself down on meadow grass next to Padmé. . . .

Stop.

He would not allow those thoughts.

For a moment he had thought of Naboo. Had almost remembered a day with Padmé.

The memories were dimmer, but they were not gone. They could still administer a fresh shot of agony if they came.

He needed Zan Arbor's memory drug. As soon as he was finished with Organa, he would head back to

Coruscant and shake that woman like a Nek battle dog with a bone until she worked day and night to perfect it.

He would get rid of the memories. And get rid of Ferus Olin. The plan was in place.

Bail turned away from the security monitor, where Darth Vader and Ferus Olin had been conferring. Too much Imperial activity on his planet. Until now the Emperor had treated him more like a pesky insect than a real threat. That had suited his purposes. But now the Empire was becoming consolidated, the Emperor had turned his eye to Alderaan. Definitely not good news.

Vader had entered the compound by using the family gate, heading straight for the private family wing. It had been done deliberately, just to let Bail know that there was nothing in this royal compound that Vader wasn't aware of. He wanted this visit to seem like an invasion.

Bail closed the panel on the security screen and left his office quickly. He decided to meet Vader head on.

He walked without hurrying toward the back rooms of the palace, the private family rooms that Vader had now polluted with his presence. He had already sent Breha to keep Leia out of sight along with the other children. He would stand between Vader and his family and his homeworld. He would not let the corruption in.

The Dark Lord lurked in the inside-outside room they used in the mornings and evenings because the blush of sunset made it glow like a flower. Bail couldn't stand the sight of him there.

"Lord Vader, if you would follow me to the reception room," he said coldly.

Vader ignored the request. "It has come to my attention that you are organizing a protest against the installation of Imperial Governors."

"It is the right of any Senator to deliver votes against measures adopted by the majority."

"You are trying to organize a voting bloc."

"And I am within my full rights to do so."

"You would not think so if you were charged with treason and thrown in an Imperial jail."

"You wouldn't dare," Bail said. "The Senate may be controlled by the Empire, but it still exists. You cannot charge a Senator with treason for following procedural rules."

"The rules have changed," Vader said.

"I haven't been informed."

"A special session is taking place at this moment. Call off your voting bloc or the treason charge will stand."

Frustration and anger roiled in Bail. No matter how he twisted and turned, the walls were closing in on him. He saw a future ahead where the Senate would cease to exist. Justice and reason would die with it.

"I should add that the Emperor sees a need for an Imperial Governor here on Alderaan."

Bail stiffened. "Alderaan has no reason for an Imperial Governor. We have a stable society. There is no risk for the Empire here. We have no weapons."

"What you have is *insubordination*. The Imperial Governor will arrive in two days."

Vader turned and left the way he had come, out through the wide doors and across the grass, cutting through the trampled garden on his way to the family gate.

Only then did Bail allow himself to tremble. He put out a hand behind him and slowly sank onto a chair.

Things were changing too fast. He was failing to see the Emperor's next step. He needed to be quicker.

He needed to confer with Mon Mothma.

He remembered the striking woman who had come to his office . . . Flame. She had been vetted by those close to him. She was the real thing. She was linking the resistance members, planet by planet. What she had done so far was impressive.

Alderaan couldn't hold out alone. He would need allies. Secret allies. Especially if they sent an Imperial Governor. Deara told him that there were those who were reconsidering the use of weapons. If there were only a few, soon there would be more.

Moonstrike could be a way out for Alderaan. A confederacy of planets would give them support. If he and the other Senators joined, it would be a political and grassroots alliance, and that could be potentially powerful. He had sent a message to Mon Mothma with Raymus Antilles, asking her to meet with Flame.

Maybe it was time he reconsidered. Maybe it was time to join Moonstrike.

CHAPTER ELEVEN

Zan Arbor had one of the apartments that took up an entire floor, in one of the upper levels of the tower. Trever stood in front of the door, running his fingers across its edges. A little discreet explosive would blast the lock. But he had to cover his tracks, too; he couldn't leave evidence that he'd been here.

He had a solution for that, a trick he'd used back on Bellassa. Tucked inside his tunic were a variety of items that would help him replace the sensor suite that locked the door. Even in high-security buildings the actual locks on the doors were usually pretty basic. The trick was not to use too much alpha charge to damage the door.

He had never exactly perfected it.

He had learned a few things from Ferus, however. One, you had to *believe* you could do the thing. Two, you had to be very, very careful. Three, you could always run.

Carefully, Trever packed his alpha charge, estimating the blast he'd need. He took out some synthblast and pushed the gummy material along the seam of the door. Then he embedded the small alpha charge in it.

He set the charge and backed up.

A small explosion, a slight puff of smoke. Sounded pretty good.

Trever bent over to examine his work. Although he was anxious to get inside, he knew he had to fix the lock now, just in case he was surprised later by someone entering the suite. He could possibly talk his way out, but not if a busted door was between him and freedom. The first mistake a thief could make was impatience.

He spread out his tools on the floor and went to work. Within three minutes he had replaced the small sensor suite that controlled the locking mechanism, sanded the metal flap, and polished it. You'd have to look very close to see the work.

He quickly replaced his tools in their pouch and fitted it inside his tunic. He was ready to search the apartment.

First he went through it, checking it out. There was a large living area with a window that overlooked the busy space lanes of Galactic City. A large terrace. He checked the mechanism and saw that the window rose into the ceiling above so that the terrace was accessible to the room. No landing platform, though. That meant she had to use one of the many semi-private ones that staggered up the building. There was a network of turbolifts that took the swells straight to their door.

All in all, pretty swanky.

There was a small, windowless room at the rear that Trever assumed could be used as a small closet or office. Instead, a bed had been moved in. He saw a maroon tunic neatly folded on top of a small table and a hair ornament with a small white stone. This was Linna Naltree's room. Naltree had saved his life when he'd been almost paralyzed with fear (okay, he could admit it now, he'd lost it) deep inside an Imperial-controlled factory in Ussa. He owed her.

He went back to the bedroom. All the cabinetry was built in flush to the wall. It didn't take him long to find Zan Arbor's datapad. This one was larger than a personal datapad, and heavier. Here was where she would keep most of her files, he guessed, accessing them when she needed to and storing them on a lighter model she would keep with her.

He flipped through the holo-directory, but all the files were coded. He didn't have Ferus or Astri's expertise, so he didn't even try to decode them. He'd hoped to find some stray piece of information that had been carelessly left unguarded — a message, a directive, anything — but he was disappointed.

Trever heard a noise from the other room that he recognized instantly — the door to the terrace had just risen. Someone must have entered the apartment without his hearing it, which was spooky because he'd kept an ear out the whole time.

Trever tugged down his cap. He'd try to get out without being seen . . . but if he was, he'd have to talk his way out. He reached for the smallest alpha charge he possessed and held it in his fingers. He'd gotten out of tough situations before by tossing the charge. The charge was so small that it didn't make a sound, but the whisper of smoke and the smell had convinced people that a small electrical fire was in progress. Trever would then pretend to be a handyman's assistant, sent to check out the problem.

Stealthily Trever tiptoed to the bedroom door. He peeked out into the living area. He didn't see anyone, but someone must be there. The large window had disappeared into the ceiling. He felt the hint of a breeze.

He waited, but he didn't hear a sound. Could the window be on a timer?

This was making him antsy.

He cautiously moved forward enough to see a little further into the room.

Nothing.

He fingered the alpha charge. Might as well use it. He tossed it gently just a few meters into the room and stepped back.

Nothing. No smoke. No smell.

It was a dud. Great.

He'd have to bluff his way out somehow. Unless there wasn't anyone out there at all. . . .

No one could be *that* quiet.

Trever moved out into the room. No one was there.

He let out the breath he was holding. He'd seen enough anyway. No need to push his luck.

He looked around for his dud alpha charge. Where had he aimed it, exactly?

He caught the shadow at his left, felt someone turning, coming out of nowhere, in full attack mode. He reached for his blaster, already knowing it was too late.

The blaster was kicked out of his hand. Trever gasped as he whirled around and saw Ry-Gaul standing in front of him, Trever's alpha charge in his large hand.

"What are you doing here?" Trever asked furiously.

Ry-Gaul's usual neutral expression didn't waver. "You first."

"Ferus asked me to monitor Zan Arbor's comings and goings —"

"This isn't monitoring. It's breaking and entering."

"I just took it one step further, that's all. I thought if I could get a look at Zan Arbor's datapad . . . well, it's coded."

"I would expect that."

"Ferus needs a plan if he wants to rescue Linna when he gets back. There's got to be a way to get her out of here."

"There is."

"How?"

Ry-Gaul moved swiftly through the room, his silver eyes taking it all in. "I don't know yet."

"Hey, your turn. Why are *you* here?"

"Tobin Gantor escaped from the Empire."

"Linna's husband?"

"Her husband and my friend. He's here on Coruscant. He contacted me. Linna managed to send him a message on a secret channel. Zen Arbor is working on a memory agent. When she perfects it, she's going to administer it to Linna as her first adult subject."

Trever let out a long whistle. "Nice way to say thanks. How close is Z.A. to the end?"

"We have no way of knowing that. But Linna thinks they're close."

"So we've got to rescue her," Trever said. "We can't risk waiting for Ferus."

"Who's *we*? I work alone."

Trever shook his head. "Not this time, you don't."

Ry-Gaul regarded him for a moment. "All right," he said. He moved back toward the bedroom again.

"So what are we doing?"

"Rule number one when you have a hostage," Ry-Gaul said. "Never follow a routine. Zan Arbor is going to arrive this evening on one of those landing platforms, and we're going to be on it. We can snatch Linna and get away. If everything goes right."

He sat down at Zan Arbor's dataport. "The work

files have layers of coding, but I'm betting the instructions on where to land are routed through the Republica tower's system. We're just going to do a little slicing into that."

"You know how to do that?"

"Jedi have many skills."

Trever watched as Ry-Gaul worked the keyboard. He pulled up a schematic of the hotel landing platforms. "That one, I think," he murmured. "Level 1010. East side. We'll have a clear shot out into a major space lane. We can get lost in the traffic." He pushed several keys. "All right then. When Zan Arbor returns, she'll have new directions telling her where to land."

"And?" Trever asked.

Ry-Gaul stood. "We'll be waiting."

CHAPTER TWELVE

Clive couldn't help it. He was enjoying himself. He'd been the one to suggest that Astri pose as his wife when they infiltrated the banking system on Niro 11. She'd known it was the best course to take, but she couldn't hide her discomfort.

It made sense to pose as a wealthy couple seeking a safe place to stash the loot they were hiding from their homeworld tax authorities. They would pass scrutiny and get into the inner sanctum of the bank, where an old source of Keets's had agreed to meet with them.

They arrived at the spaceport in a driving rain. They had already been cleared while onboard the luxury class cruiser and were immediately whisked aboard a private air shuttle with a uniformed pilot. As soon as they were seated he pressed a lever and a tray slid out with a variety of refreshments.

"Help yourselves," he said. "We'll be at Bank Niro Eleven in twelve point two minutes."

Clive leaned back against the cushy upholstery. "I could get used to this. Hey — I'm *already* used to it."

Astri looked tensely out the window at the streaming rain. "Being rich is not all it's cracked up to be."

"Oh, that's right, you were married to a politician," Clive said. "Must have been an easy life."

"Easy," Astri repeated. She turned her dark eyes on Clive and gave him a look of such sadness that it stopped the jest on his lips.

They said nothing for the remainder of the ride. They sped over an icy gray sea, so vast they couldn't see the edges of it, and headed for a cluster of tall buildings, each with a differently colored spire at the top.

"Your meeting is in Building Yellow," the driver said. "An escort will be at the landing platform. Have a pleasant stay."

He piloted the craft to a smooth landing on a landing platform under a canopy. Not a drop of rain touched them as they exited. An escort waited, a tall, angular woman in a long white tunic. She inclined her head.

"Mr. and Mrs. Telstarr," she said. "Herk Bloomi is expecting you."

She led them to a turbolift and it rose swiftly. Clive looked at the levels flash. It stopped on level three hundred and ten.

They stepped out to a panoramic view of silver lake and gray sky. Up here the rain had turned to hardened crystals that tapped on the transparisteel. They were led to a plush couch and left there. The air was cold and Astri shivered.

"I don't like this place," she said. "There's a bad feeling here."

"It's the feeling of those who have too much and want to keep it all to themselves," Clive said.

Moments later a plump, fastidious older man entered. His bald head shone and his boots gleamed with polish. "Mr. and Mrs. Telstarr. Pleased to meet you. Herk Bloomi, director of new accounts at Bank Niro."

"Pleased to meet you, mate. We're looking for a safe place to stash our considerable fortune," Clive said. "Just what you like to hear, eh?"

"Just a moment. I'll activate the privacy booth. Our clients feel more secure that way."

He waved his hand over a sensor and curved transparent walls lowered around them, encasing them in a small room within the room. He pressed a button and the walls acquired a shimmer.

"We can see out but no one can see in. And this blocks surveillance devices. Complete privacy, but we should be brief," Herk said.

"Thank you for seeing us," Astri said. "Keets Freely said that you'd agreed to help."

"I am a banker," Bloomi said. "A banker believes in certain things. The sanctity of wealth. The right to privacy. I don't agree with what the Empire is doing. The financial future of the galaxy depends on the right of the wealthy to protect their accounts. We are now asked to hand over details of deposits and withdrawals on a weekly basis to an Imperial investigator." He shuddered. "It's a terrible thing."

Clive couldn't believe it. The Empire was smashing whole societies and this guy was worried about some fat rat's pile of credits?

Astri shot him a look that told him to be quiet. She leaned forward and asked softly, "So you'll help us?"

He licked his lips nervously. "Keets said that you needed details on only one account. . . ."

"Only one. It will help us enormously," Astri said. "You'll be doing a great service to the galaxy."

"The Empire's disregard for rules offends me," he said. "That's the only reason I would violate a client's privacy . . . and you say that you are trying to help this person. . . ."

"Absolutely, mate," Clive said. "It's life or death. And money."

"All right then." Bloomi pressed a button on his armrest and a small datapad slid out. He tapped the keys. "Yarrow Industries moved their accounts off-world near the end of the Clone Wars."

"Who moved the accounts?" Clive asked.

"At first, Evin Yarrow, the chief officer of Yarrow Industries. After his death, his daughter Eve completed the transfer. It was under Imperial order. That happened to many of our clients around that time."

"So even though the Empire moved the account, she still controlled it?"

"Oh, very much so. She asked that we key the Yarrow account to numbers instead of names. We also wiped all evidence of ties to Acherin."

"Is the account still active?" Astri asked, even though she knew the answer.

"Oh, yes. Regular payouts." Bloomi checked the screen. "As a matter of fact, the payouts have been increasing of late."

"Where do the credits transfer to?" Clive asked.

"A numbered account on Revery. Do you know the planet? Many of our clients have homes there."

Clive nodded. He'd never been there, but he'd certainly heard of Revery. It was a noted haunt for the super-rich. It was known for its beaches and mountains . . . and also for its privacy.

"Can you get us Eve Yarrow's coordinates on Revery?" Clive asked.

"No," Bloomi said, his head bent. "No, that's not accessible. Addresses are strictly private."

"But you said that the Empire violates the privacy of your clients," Astri said. "That they cross-check numbers with names . . . so if they do that, you must have the information in your files."

Clever girl, Clive thought.

"I told you, there's only so far I can go," Bloomi said. He raised his head. Clive saw fear in his eyes. "I gave you the planet — isn't that enough?"

Astri hesitated. "Suppose we were clients of yours, and we needed a moment to confer? Couldn't you step out of the privacy room and leave us for a moment? And maybe forget to close the datapad?"

The decision weighed in his eyes.

"If we promise to never ask you for information again," Astri added.

Clive wanted to lean on the guy, but he knew it would be a mistake. Finally Bloomi pushed himself off the couch with his balled fists. "I, uh, need to check on something."

He pressed a button and the transparent wall slid back. Clearing his throat nervously, he slid out. The wall slid back.

Astri quickly revolved the datapad so she could see it. She clicked on the keys. "He left the coded files open to his security code. Good man. Here's the transaction list . . . if I just jump to the numbered file contact info . . . yes," Astri murmured, satisfied. "Memorize these coordinates." Softly she read out the numbers.

Clive nodded. "Got it."

Astri looked out. The room was empty. "Well, as long as I'm here. . . ." She clicked a few more keys, searching.

"What are you looking for?"

"I don't know. Anything out of the ordinary. I —"

Suddenly Clive saw Bloomi enter the room with several Imperial officers. "Close it," he said softly, even though he knew they couldn't hear.

Astri quickly shut the datapad as the wall rose.

There was now a sheen of perspiration on Bloomi's high forehead. "Mr. and Mrs. Telstarr, we have a security check. Strictly routine."

Clive admired Astri's coolness. Posing as a rich woman, she put on an irritated look. "Do they know who we *are*?" she hissed at the banker.

"Strictly routine, madam," Bloomi answered. Clive noted that his hands were shaking. "It will take only a moment."

"Now, angel hair, let's not hold up these gentlemen," Clive said. "This is the price we pay for a secure galaxy. Here you go, sirs." He handed over his ID doc and motioned for Astri to do the same.

With a slight pursing of her lips, she did so.

Clive waited while the lead officer scanned their docs through his datapad. He wished he could dump a bucket of ice water on Bloomi's head. The bloke was now sweating profusely, his collar damp and the few strands of hair he possessed now plastered to his scalp.

Astri waited with the air of a woman who did not like to wait. Her training as a Senator's wife obviously came in handy.

The check went on for too long. Clive saw the moment the Imperial officer registered that something was amiss.

"If you'll wait here for just another moment," he said.

"Our business is concluded," Astri said. "We were just leaving."

"I'm sorry, I'll have to insist." The officer's tone was still polite. He couldn't afford to alienate them if they really were the fabulously wealthy Telstarrs.

Which they weren't. Maybe the real Telstarrs had noticed that someone was using their ID docs. Even though Curran had used his best contact for the docs, you could never trust the black market completely.

They were in trouble.

The officers moved off to confer. Probably waiting for a superior to tell them what to do.

"Do you think they know?" Bloomi wiped his forehead with his sleeve. "Do you think so?"

"Do you have a cruiser with a hyperdrive?" Clive asked him in a low tone.

"Of course. In my business you need the best . . . wait a moment. You're not suggesting. . . ."

"Give me the security code. We'll try to get it back to you if we can. Sometime."

"You can't just . . . leave!"

"I'm afraid we have to. In another minute, that officer is going to get an order to arrest us." Clive kept a pleasant smile on his face and leaned back on the couch as though he didn't have a care in the world.

"If that happens, they might arrest you, too," Astri said. "But if you give us your cruiser, we'll make it look like we stole it from you. You can claim innocence."

"Just don't tell them who we were investigating, no matter what," Clive warned.

Bloomi wrung his hands. "I don't know what to do."

"Look natural," Astri said through her smile. "Tell me the code."

He told them the code they'd need and where to find the speeder. "But how are you going to get to the turbolift?"

"Leave that to us."

"You're not going to use blasters, are you?"

Clive rose smoothly. "My advice? Duck."

"Let me go first," Astri told him, and before he could protest she walked toward the officers.

"This is absurd," she said. "Our liner is about to depart. I demand to see your superior officer!"

"We really must be going," Clive said, taking Astri by the elbow.

The officer stepped forward. "Sir, you can't go —"

They kept moving toward the turbolift. The officer was nervous now. There was still a chance that the ID doc confusion was just a snag in communications. He was reluctant to take responsibility for attacking them.

"We'll be available at the spaceport," Clive said. "We're on the luxury liner *Iridescence*."

"We can clear up any confusion before departure," Astri said. "Send your superior to our stateroom."

Clive closed the remaining distance to the turbolift and hit the sensor.

The officer finally realized he had to do something or risk a long term as a security officer on a mining planet. He drew his blaster. "Stop right there."

"Don't be silly," Clive said, taking a step back toward them. "I'm sure we can work this out. . . ."

The turbolift opened.

Clive and Astri drew their blasters. They fired at the lights overhead and the sensor suite that controlled the transparent partitions. The partitions descended all at the same time. The officer's blasterfire went awry. It pinged off the transparent walls and ricocheted around the room.

Astri and Clive jumped into the turbolift. It descended swiftly.

"We have maybe a minute before they figure this out," Clive said. "Be prepared to run."

They burst off the turbolift as it opened onto the private landing platform. They found Bloomi's cruiser parked near the lip of the platform. Clive jumped in. Astri blasted the security console next to the cruiser.

"They won't be able to tell we had the code," she said. "Bloomi might escape detection that way."

Stormtroopers suddenly pounded through the entrance. Clive powered up the engines as Astri somersaulted away past the worst of the fire, jumped up on the back of the cruiser, and scrambled for the open cockpit. "Go!" she screamed above the sound of blasterfire.

She leaped in the cockpit, still firing, as he pushed the engines. They screamed out into the sky. Clive hit the upper atmosphere and then space. He could see Imperial fighters heading after them. Cannonfire streaked toward them.

"Hyperspace coming up," he said. "Hang on."

In a rush of stars, they evaded the fighters.

"That was close," Clive said.

"Can we trust Bloomi not to talk?" Astri asked, tucking her blaster back in her belt. "If he does, we'll find an Imperial attack ship as we come out of hyperspace at Revery."

"Do I trust Herk?" Clive shook his head. "No. All they have to do is show him a picture of a torture droid and he'll cave. But maybe they won't ask him the right questions. Maybe they'll just assume we were your ordinary bank robbers."

"We could always go back to Coruscant," Astri said.

They exchanged a look.

Astri leaned forward. "Onward to Revery," she said.

CHAPTER THIRTEEN

Ferus closed his comlink. Obi-Wan wasn't responding on the emergency channel. What could he be doing? Herding banthas?

He continued on his way. He had donned the Inquisitor robe again, hating it, but knowing it could help him. He was heading for the spaceport. He could only hope that the letters and numbers scrawled in the dust had something to do with what the spy had seen through the electrobinoculars.

He had a feeling that Obi-Wan had known very well that the Force-adept he was chasing was Bail's daughter. It explained why he was here. But what else did Obi-Wan know that he wasn't telling?

Ferus hadn't seen Darth Vader since that morning at the palace, but he could feel him. Not through the Force, but through an instinct that his enemy was occupying space near him. Ferus touched the hidden pocket where the Sith Holocron nestled. His lungs burned. He took a ragged breath. He felt as though he were falling into a black hole, slowly, while familiar faces, people he loved, homes he'd lived in, places he'd enjoyed were all around him as he spun past them, unable to touch them, unable to connect.

His salvation could be this small object in his pocket. Grief had not only sapped his power, but his purpose; the Force could restore it, but not the Force he knew.

He took his hand away. He no longer knew which thoughts were coming from him and which were under the influence of the Holocron. That scared him, but it thrilled him deeply, too. He knew he should throw the Holocron away, toss it in the deepest point of the great lake of Alderaan. . . .

You cannot throw it away. It is yours now. By accepting it, you own it. You have already begun the journey. Soon you will recognize it.

Whose voice was that?

Ferus rubbed his forehead. He had felt the voice as part of himself, deeper than his own voice. Did it speak truth or lies? What was happening to him?

His comlink buzzed, and he snatched it from his belt. It was Hydra.

"Checking in."

"Nothing to report on this end," Ferus said. "How's the document search going?"

"I'm getting full cooperation now. Lord Vader's presence on the planet has helped us. They're worried about an Imperial takeover. We have *fear* working for us now." Hydra's flat monotone held the tinge of satisfaction.

"Well, keep going. Contact me if you learn anything." Ferus ended the communication.

He was racing the clock now. He didn't think Hydra would learn anything about Leia at the documents office, but she would soon give that up and look a different way. He had to discount the rumor before Hydra found the girl.

And, in the meantime, he had to find the Imperial spy.

He took the turbolift up to the busy spaceport. Vehicles lined up for takeoff and refueling. The command center was in a round building off to the side. Ferus approached, throwing back his hood slightly.

When he entered, the busy workers looked up, then quickly looked down. They wouldn't want to give him any information, but they'd have to. He wished he could tell them he was on their side.

He went up to the woman who looked as though she was in charge. "I have an information request," he said.

"We're busy here." Her voice was curt, but her eyes were scared.

"I just need to identify this vehicle. The spaceport code is LCS79244-12u712."

"That's not a vehicle code."

"Then what is it?" he asked.

She pressed her lips together. For a moment he thought she'd refuse.

"Would you rather Lord Vader came here to enquire?" he asked. He hated to push that way, but he had to know.

She looked down. "It's a product entry code," she said. "LCS means Load Coded and Shipped. That means that a delivery came into the spaceport and we shipped it out again."

"Then you must have the address where it was shipped."

She turned toward the console. "I'll plug it in. But I can tell you right now, the destination code is wrong. First of all, there aren't enough numbers."

Ferus remembered the smudge. Some of the numbers must have been wiped out.

"Second, there are no letters in the destination code. I know it was shipped to Aldera — the code is twelve. But the rest of it doesn't make sense."

"See what you can do."

She called up the list of shipments. "I can't find it." She looked at him defensively. "See for yourself." She tilted the screen toward him. "We get hundreds of shipments. Your numbers don't make sense in terms of the system."

Ferus studied the screen. She wasn't lying. It would be impossible to trace without the correct sequence of numbers.

He turned away, frustrated. At least he knew it was a shipment the spy had been looking at. Or maybe heard about . . . there was no way to know.

He couldn't leave the planet until he had answers. He couldn't leave the Organas at the mercy of the Empire. Something was going on here. The knowledge of it was deep in his bones. He had to keep looking.

He spent the night at the temporary quarters that had been arranged for him, and woke before dawn. He decided that if he searched the warehouse again, he might come across something he'd overlooked.

It was still dark as he made his way across the deserted park. The warehouses loomed ahead, dark sentinels overlooking the square of green.

He was crossing toward the warehouse when he saw it.

"If you want to get lucky, open your eyes."
Thank you, Siri!

Crouched between the taller warehouses and hangars, Ferus saw an old, decrepit building he hadn't noticed before. It was built of old stone, bleached and pockmarked from hundreds of years of duty. It was only about ten stories, and appeared abandoned.

Above the doorway there were numbers chiseled into the stone in the old style. Crumbling, darkened with age, hard to read, but there.

8712

He thought back to the "u" he thought he had seen. Maybe it had been the lower part of the number 8. Part of it had been wiped away.

Could it be this easy? Could the shipment have been sent across the street from the spy's overlook?

Why not? If you wanted to keep tabs on a shipment, what better place could there be?

Ferus crossed back and carefully examined the building as he walked past. He did it without seeming to look, keeping his head forward and striding purposefully. Even though the area was deserted he knew that there could be night workers about in the surrounding buildings. Even the spy could be at his post this early, though spaceport traffic was light.

In the short time it took to walk by, he was able to spot the security panel and identify it as one he recognized. Very high-tech, considering the building.

He turned at the corner and went down the block, past the backs of the warehouses. Many of them had landing platforms, but the smaller warehouse did not. A high security fence surrounded it, most likely with some sort of electroshock capacity.

The street was deserted. Ferus gathered the Force and leaped. He sailed over the fence easily and landed in the backyard of the warehouse, a small area of crumbling permacrete.

There was one small durasteel door. The same

security panel. Ferus had no problem bypassing the code. He heard the lock click.

He pushed open the door and walked inside to a small hallway. There was no turbolift, just a curving ramp leading upward. The lighting was dim. He approached slowly, listening for sounds. He heard a soft *whirr* and quickly pressed himself into the shadows. A surveillance droid flew by slowly, rotating as it went. It had a visual field, not infrared, so if he stayed out of sight he'd be all right.

Ferus walked up the ramp to the first floor. He could see that he was in a large open space. Rusted speeder parts were dumped in piles along the walls. An old system of automated pulleys hung from the ceiling, parts dangling, rusty and coated with dirt. He walked back and forth, looking carefully, but didn't find anything but more old parts and tools.

Not too promising, so far. Evading the droids, he searched the next level, and the next. Finally he reached the top floor. He looked overhead. He could see the mechanism for a retractable roof. That would be how shipments could be moved in and out. There was plenty of room here to land a small barge. If the operation was done at night, the offloading could be quick and close to private in the middle of a city.

At first this floor looked like the others. But as he walked closer, Ferus saw the duratsteel bins stacked up against the walls.

New durasteel.

Ferus got down on his haunches. He saw the airport code stenciled on one side.

LCS226579244 12 8712

SPEEDER PARTS was stamped on the side.

He ran his hand along the top. It was unsealed. Cautiously, he pulled open the top.

The bin was empty.

Ferus went from bin to bin. They were all empty. He crouched down and began to examine the floor underneath the roof. He took out his tiny glowlight and ran it over the floor.

Yes. A craft had landed here recently. He saw the scorch marks, the scratches.

He stayed in that position for long minutes, thinking.

He was so deep in thought he didn't hear the soft footsteps until they were coming up the last turn of the ramp. Someone trying very, very hard to be quiet.

Ferus dashed for cover as the room suddenly lit up with blasterfire. He dived to the floor and rolled, cursing his inattention. He rolled to safety behind a partially dismantled airspeeder. The blasterfire pinged. He smelled hot metal.

He ran behind a pile of dismantled parts. The blasterfire followed him. Ferus had run in order to assess. Now he knew that his pursuer was a good shot. Good information to have when you're trapped.

Ferus considered what to do. He would have to escape without using his lightsaber. If he were being attacked by the Imperial spy — and chances were pretty much one hundred percent that he was — the information would get back to the Emperor. Ferus didn't relish having to explain why, as a supposed Imperial Inquisitor, he was investigating a mystery shipment being tracked by an Imperial spy. But worse than that, any Force activity on this planet would only throw the spotlight more clearly on it. Ferus needed to divert the Emperor's attention from Alderaan, not attract it.

What he needed was a push-back. Something that would send his assailant running so that he could trail him.

Ferus leaped above to the rack and pulley system that still held old parts and engines. He crawled forward and found the mechanism that moved the parts forward on an automatic track. He activated it.

Now the rack moved forward, jerking slightly as it went. The noise brought the attention of the shooter, and blasterfire streaked through the air, hitting behind Ferus now as the rack moved forward. Ferus released an airspeeder engine. It smashed to the floor. Then a windscreen. Engine parts. A halfway dismantled pit droid. Sparks flew upward as the metal screeched against the permacrete floor.

The rack kept moving, faster now, on the fastest speed that Ferus could locate, and he balanced on the pulley, moving forward and dropping parts and engines and heavy sheets of metal as it went. It was tricky to keep his balance on the pulley as it jerked along, but he managed it.

The space was now full of the sound of crashing metal, and Ferus tracked the shadow as it moved, trying to get a fix on him. Ferus's aim was to corner him, but he was moving so fluidly and the pulley system just wasn't fast enough.

If only he was strong enough in the Force to give the heavy objects a little *push.*

Within his tunic he felt the Holocron glow.

You are forgetting what your rage can do.

His irritation at the spy surprising him was just a spark, something he had accepted and released. It had been so unimportant. It got in the way of Jedi battle-mind.

He revived it. Fanned it.

His anger grew.

How dare he interfere with me?

He, just a low-level spy. He thinks he's going to win. He is nothing.

The next airspeeder part didn't just crash to the floor. It flew through the air with great velocity, smashing over the shadow's head. Ferus fed his anger until it balled up into rage and shot out into the space, taking the machinery and parts and flinging them toward the hiding places of the spy.

Satisfaction coursed through him. Thoughts of forcing the spy to flee and tailing him vanished. *I can smash him I can kill him I can destroy him. . . .*

He saw the shadow moving toward the door, a tall, thin figure that seemed familiar. How remarkable that even through the red haze of his anger his perceptions could be so sharp. . . .

You see? You use the anger. It does not confuse. It sharpens.

The spy ran out toward the ramp.

Ferus jumped from the pulleys. He leaped over the piles of smoking metal.

His mind cooled. He saw even as he ran how thoroughly he had destroyed this space.

He didn't feel satisfaction anymore. He felt unsettled. Guilty. He pushed away the feeling. He would deal with it all later. Now it was time to track the spy.

Ferus ran down the ramp, running fast but not fast enough to risk letting the spy know he was being followed. He would assume that it would take some time for Ferus to fight his way through the machinery piled on the floor in the hangar above. He wouldn't imagine that Ferus would be on his heels.

He followed the spy down the ramp, down below street level. Ferus wanted to kick himself. He hadn't done such a good job of reconnoitering after all. The buildings were linked by an underground passage.

The passage was dimly lit and wide enough for the biggest gravsled to operate. Ferus could hear the spy's progress and tracked him through his footsteps. He had slowed down now, assuming he hadn't been followed. Ferus followed him in the passage for about a kilometer. Then he hopped aboard a turbolift. Ferus looked up at the indicator. He'd gotten off at street level. He counted out a few seconds and then followed.

Ferus emerged into a surprisingly busy street. Dawn was just beginning to streak the sky with orange. He saw gravsleds and utility ramps set up down at the end of the street. He realized that an open-air market was being set up right under the shadow of the spaceport.

Ferus followed the activity into the market. It must have been a permanent fixture, for the large square was filled with stalls that marched in winding rows. The partitions were made of heavy durasteel poles and brightly colored awnings. Open bins held piles of items.

The day's unloading was taking place — vegetables and fruits, baked goods, household items, robes, cloths, plants, flowers, tools. The merchants chatted in small groups, or busily set up their stalls.

Ferus made his way through the crowd, looking for the figure he'd chased. He felt sure he'd recognize him by his height and the way he moved, even though he hadn't seen his face.

Instead, he bumped into Deara. A basket filled with

fruit and muffins was on her arm. She moved her basket to her other arm, as though she couldn't trust him not to steal it.

"Just enjoying the bounty of your planet," he said, gesturing to the stalls around him.

Her face flushed. "It seems your Empire believes that our bounty is yours for the taking." As if afraid she'd said too much, she quickly walked away.

Ferus stood in the middle of the market. Around him was food he could not reach for and people who despised him.

Inside his tunic was a dark future. A path lay before him that all his life he had known was wrong.

He had wanted to kill that spy. Just as Vader had killed Roan, for no good reason except he was in his way.

If he killed Vader using the same kind of power, would that turn him into just another version of the Dark Lord?

Ferus pressed his chest with his hand, felt his heartbeat. He saw everything ahead of him, all the wrong he could do. He was being pulled along that path.

Why couldn't he stop himself?

CHAPTER FOURTEEN

Ry-Gaul and Trever waited at the landing platform all afternoon for Zan Arbor to return. They knew she varied her routine and could return at any time. Waiting wasn't too hard. It was *where* they had to wait that was the problem.

It happened to be behind the exhaust grille of a star yacht, but they didn't have a choice. There was no other place to conceal themselves on the platform. The exhaust grille was hot. It was cramped. It smelled. Still, Ry-Gaul and Trever lay curled against the metal for hours.

And Ry-Gaul wasn't the most thrilling conversationalist. All Trever was able to get out of him was, "Later or soon, it will happen."

Thanks.

As the sunset painted the windows of the tower bright orange, Ry-Gaul stirred. Zan Arbor's transport appeared, a top of the line airspeeder in brushed chromium. She made no attempt at disguise. She drove the luxury speeder with the roof retracted, looping once around the crowded plaza below to show herself off.

Trever nudged Ry-Gaul. "Linna's in the back."

The Jedi nodded, his pale gray eyes never leaving the sight. Zan Arbor dipped the craft and moved smoothly down to land on the platform.

As Zan Arbor gathered her things to depart, Ry-Gaul leaped out of the exhaust grille and slid underneath the belly of the star yacht. Trever followed. They waited while Zan Arbor exited, followed by Linna.

They had already decided to grab Linna in the small reception room that lay beyond the entrance. There, occupants at the hotel could take off their outer garments and access turbolifts to take them to their private apartments.

Zan Arbor and Linna disappeared inside. Trever and Ry-Gaul followed. They found themselves in a small reception area with hammered azurite walls.

From an open doorway ahead they could hear Zan Arbor giving loud orders to a fussing protocol droid. "Take this cape and press it. And no, I do *not* want the chaughaine tonight. How many times have I told you? The emerald satina — I'm going to the opera."

Ry-Gaul signaled to Trever. It was time to alert Linna that they were ready to take her away.

They started forward, but Ry-Gaul suddenly put his

hand on Trever's shoulder to stop him. He leaned over and whispered, "Trouble."

Instead of heading toward Zan Arbor, Ry-Gaul turned to the turbolift.

He accessed it and entered with Trever on his heels. The turbolift was the size of a small room, with gilt walls and a plush floorcovering.

"Uh, this seems to be a no-way-out situation to me," Trever offered.

Ry-Gaul held onto the side rails, kicked out, and supported himself upside down while he kicked up at the roof panel.

He caught the panel with one hand when it fell and yet managed at the same time to push himself through, upside down. Trever threw his head back, peering up into the blackness. He'd never seen such a display of agility. "Wow," he said. "Are you —"

His words were choked off as Ry-Gaul's feet came down, grabbed him around his shoulders, and yanked him upward. Trever was whisked through the opening and landed hard on the top of the turbolift. He was about to protest but Ry-Gaul motioned him to be quiet as he silently slid the roof panel back in place.

Trever shot him a questioning look. What could be more trouble than sitting on top of an express turbolift that no doubt went extremely fast, waiting for a crazy genius evil scientist to enter it?

Then he knew. He heard the rasp of the breathing. Darth Vader.

Zan Arbor's voice sounded petulant as they entered the turbolift. "I didn't know you were back in Imperial City, but I'm glad to have a chance to talk to you. You promised me more human subjects."

"You promised me progress."

"I have made tremendous progress. It's all in my reports. But I still need adult subjects."

"You have done enough research. It is time to produce the agent."

"I don't have time for this. I have tickets to the opera tonight. I'm meeting Senator Sauro."

"Let us step inside. I am not finished."

The turbolift rose swiftly. Trever turned slightly to look up to the end of the shaft. At this rate they should reach it in less than a minute. He wondered how much room there was between the elevator roof and the ceiling of the shaft.

"I am a perfectionist," Zan Arbor said. "That is the reason you hired me, correct? It's hardly the time to push me, now that we're so close to the end."

"This is *exactly* the time," Vader thundered. "You are too cautious!"

"I am a scientist!"

"You are a coward!"

Ry-Gaul cocked his head, listening intently.

"Did you come here just to rant at me? I can contact

the Emperor, you know. He might be interested in your . . . strange urgency."

Ry-Gaul was now listening intently, his eyes closed.

Suddenly the turbolift shuddered, then reversed.

"What are you doing? You didn't even touch the sensor. . . ."

"I have done what I came to do. I will be back tomorrow, when I will want to hear a plan to have the memory agent online within the month."

Trever held onto the turbolift as it zoomed downward. It seemed to be going awfully fast.

"I demand you slow this turbolift down, Lord Vader." Zan Arbor's voice shook. "If this is a display of your Force-ability, I hardly need it. I am an expert, you know."

"The fact that you consider yourself an expert," Vader said, "only proves how *ignorant* you are."

The turbolift stopped with a violent jerk, as if it had smashed into ground, not air. The only thing that prevented Trever from tumbling off into the shaft was Ry-Gaul's strong grip. He heard a scramble below; bodies falling.

"You will hear about this, Lord Vader!" Zan Arbor screeched.

They heard the doors open and the sound of his boots, followed by the scuffling sounds of someone trying to rise, and panting.

"He's going to pay for that," Zan Arbor said. "Get this thing moving, Linna. Fast!"

"I think the sensor might be broken —"

"Just do it!"

Ry-Gaul signaled to Trever. Now was the time. Zan Arbor was already off balance from her confrontation with Vader.

Ry-Gaul went first, slipping down into the turbolift in one fluid movement. Trever followed.

He cannonballed into the space. His job was to protect Linna while Ry-Gaul took care of Zan Arbor. As he landed, his foot tangled in a thick chaughaine cape that Zan Arbor must have left on the floor. He lost his balance and fell. Linna reached out for him.

Zan Arbor took out a small deadly blaster. Linna was now exposed.

The look of triumph in Zan Arbor's eyes was erased when Ry-Gaul charged, his lightsaber held in a defensive posture.

Linna had already leaped forward to protect Trever, pulling something from her med pack. Trever yelled, afraid that the blasterfire would hit her despite Ry-Gaul's lightsaber.

Zan Arbor, her lips drawn back in a smile, peppered Ry-Gaul with blasterfire. Trever hit the ground as the fire ricocheted around the turbolift. Linna hit the floor, too, and Zan Arbor turned, aiming the blaster at her.

Linna reached forward and pressed a delivery

syringe full of a blue-gray liquid into Zan Arbor's ankle.

Zan Arbor screamed and dropped her blaster. She writhed, falling to the ground, and beat her head against the floor. She reached for Linna, who drew back.

"No!" Zan Arbor screamed. "No!"

"What did you do?" Trever whispered to Linna.

Ry-Gaul clipped his lightsaber back onto his belt. "She gave her the memory agent."

Linna leaned over Zan Arbor. She spoke clearly and quietly, with no menace in her voice. Only resolve.

"You will never use your brilliance to hurt people again."

Zan Arbor put her hands to her head. "The formula . . . I'm losing it. Tell it to me!"

Linna was silent. She waved her hand over the sensor and the turbolift began to rise.

"The interactions of chemicals with organic substance . . . the formula for toxic delivery systems by water . . ." Zan Arbor began to pull at her hair. "It's gone! My experiments! I can't remember them!"

She crashed back against the wall.

"My training! My genius!"

Trever watched as panic raced across her face. "The Bibinger formula!" she screamed. "My work with the transmission of plague element . . . it's gone! Chemical equations . . . the amount of weight times gravity times . . . times . . ."

"It was a full dose," Linna murmured. "Not targeted. I'm not sure how it will affect her, but I think at the very least she'll lose all her scientific training . . . fifty years' worth . . ."

"Who are you?" Zan Arbor suddenly turned to Linna. "I don't know you."

The doors slid open. Linna led her out into the sumptuous apartment.

"I don't know this place!"

"This is your home."

Linna walked over to Zan Arbor's datapad. She slipped it under her arm.

"You did this to me," Zan Arbor said suddenly, looking at Linna. "I remember enough to know I was a genius. Now I'm a nobody! I'm a nobody!"

Linna walked back into the turbolift.

"You might as well have killed me!" Zan Arbor shrieked.

The turbolift doors closed, and they descended. All the way down they heard her screams.

CHAPTER FIFTEEN

Hydra contacted Ferus as he was leaving the open-air market. Her voice was curt.

"There's been a break in the investigation. I discovered there was a weather forecasting satellite overhead on the day in question. The findings include ground photos. They are wiped at the end of each day. So they said. But I went into the computers and found a cache with old information. Found the day in question."

Ferus felt his heart fall. "That's good news."

"Unfortunately whatever the incident was, I can't locate it. The satellite only covers a portion of the park during the time in question. But I was able to cross-check with airspeeder ID tags. We'll miss out on those who arrived on foot but if we squeeze the others for names we'll really be getting somewhere. We'll have almost everyone who was in the park that day. I can interview all of them."

This was exactly what he didn't want to happen.

"I'll sit in," he said.

"If you must."

He got the distinct impression when he disconnected that she was either exasperated at his incompetence or suspected his loyalty. Neither was a good sign.

Sitting in on interviews with Alderaan citizens with Hydra gave Ferus a close-up look at dignity and fear.

Dignity: The Alderaanians detested them but treated them with courtesy.

Fear: The Alderaanians knew the Inquisitors had the power to throw them in an Imperial prison without trial or charges.

Hydra was good at her job. He watched the way she inspected the dwellings, her gaze lingering on family holo-photos, the way she asked detailed questions about the ages of the children. She held their fear in her hands and squeezed.

The interviews made Ferus feel ill. *I need to stop doing this. I'm not cut out for it.*

The Sith Holocron whispered in his head, in his own voice, *You underestimate your ability to be cruel.*

By the end of the day, Hydra was barely concealing her fury. None of the Alderaanians gave up a single name of anyone they knew at the park. They all claimed that the park was too crowded, they didn't know anyone that day, or maybe they would provide a first name, a common name that would be impossible to trace. Hydra even interviewed the children and drew the same response. It was obvious that the children had been prepared as well as the adults.

It reminded him of the solidarity and courage of the resistance on his homeworld of Bellassa. It made him proud.

Hydra checked her data list at the end of the day. "I can always do a second round of interviews. Maybe start detentions off-planet."

"I don't think this warrants it," Ferus said. "Let me see the list." He checked over the names that Hydra had compiled. "You missed a name," he said. "Sona Ziemba." He would have let it pass, but it wasn't like Hydra to overlook something. Why had she?

She glanced at it. He saw no expression on her face. "Let's check it out."

Sona Ziemba lived in a large apartment block nearby. The building was in a crowded neighborhood of workers. It was the time of workers going home, of preparations for the evening meal, of the satisfaction of a day well spent, and Ferus felt his own isolation even more keenly as life swirled around him. He was apart from all this now.

There is nothing here for you to miss. Ordinary life is nothing.

No, ordinary life was everything.

You are kidding yourself. Recognize that and begin a more important journey.

His thoughts were so loud he wondered if Hydra could hear them.

They took a turbolift up to the fifty-third floor. They rang the bell at the apartment and a pretty woman answered the door. A dark-haired girl raced behind her, chasing a toy. To his surprise, Ferus recognized them. He'd seen them the very first day. The girl's name was Tula.

The woman's face froze when she saw their Inquisitor's cloaks.

"Sona Ziemba?"

Slowly, the woman nodded. Her eyes darted from Hydra to Ferus.

"I am Imperial Inquisitor Hydra, and this is Head Inquisitor Ferus Olin. We have a few questions for you regarding your presence in Grasslands Park one week ago Thursday."

Hydra walked past her, not waiting for the woman to invite her in. Ferus followed.

"Were you there on that day?"

"I'm there every day." Sona Ziemba swallowed. "With my daughter. My husband and I had a business, and it failed. And my mother . . . she used to take care of Tula, and she died last fall . . . so I take her there every day. . . ."

Ferus recognized the signs of someone giving more information than needed because they were nervous.

"Did you know about the incident where someone almost fell into the sea when a barrier wall gave way?" Hydra asked.

"I didn't see it."

"But you know about it?"

"Some of the mothers and fathers were talking about it, yes. We talk . . ."

Hydra whipped out her datapad. "Can you give me names?"

A slight hesitation alerted Ferus that the woman was about to lie. "I don't know their names. Just the other parents. We just chat sometimes. We don't ask each other's names."

Hydra made a notation.

The door opened behind them. A tall, thin man walked in, his arm filled with a basket of food.

Again, Ferus was surprised. He had seen that man the first day at the park, through his electrobinoculars. Now he realized why the shadowy spy looked familiar. They were the same.

"Dartan!" Sona said with relief. "You're home. These are Imperial Inquisitors. They're asking about Grasslands . . . something that happened there."

"Strictly routine," Hydra said.

Ferus felt the back of his neck prickle. Hydra had

given the man an *It's all right* signal. She'd hidden it well, but he had seen it. Hydra knew the man was a spy. And Ferus was guessing that the man's wife did not.

That was why Hydra hadn't bothered to investigate this woman. There was no need. If Sona Ziemba had known something, she would have told her husband. And it would have gone straight into his report.

Looking around the tiny apartment, Ferus felt a rush of sympathy. This family didn't have much. The wife had lost her job.

Dartan put the basket down. Ferus recognized food from the market. Perhaps Dartan worked there.

No doubt he had been corrupted by the idea of wealth for his family. That's how many spies were recruited. *Just keep your eyes and ears open,* the Imperial recruiter would say in a friendly way. *You don't have to betray your neighbors. Just give us bits of information.*

And so the person would pass along something, then another thing, and before he knew it he was compromised. He would be asked to do more and more until he found himself on top of a warehouse building with electrobinoculars trained on the main spaceport. And then there was no turning back.

One day he would realize that he'd betrayed not only his neighbors, but everything he believed in.

Now Ferus knew how it happened. Dartan had been bored with the spaceport, had turned his electrobinoculars down to the park to seek out his wife and daughter . . . and had seen the incident with Leia. He had reported it because he had nothing else.

"You work at the market?" Ferus asked.

Dartan nodded.

"Have a good evening," Hydra said. "We'll contact you again if we need to."

As they descended to street level, Hydra spoke. "An Imperial Governor will be arriving tomorrow," she said with satisfaction. "Organa forced the Emperor to take a stand here. It was a stupid move to send Antilles fleeing when Lord Vader arrived. Did he think the Empire's reach didn't extend to TerraAsta?" She snorted. "So much for his so-called intellect. Alderaan will soon discover that it can't operate if it doesn't cooperate with us."

Ferus walked out into the soft evening air. His mind buzzed with the information Hydra had just dropped.

Dartan Ziemba couldn't have reported that Raymus Antilles had left Alderaan. He had left secretly. Bail had sent Raymus Antilles to the TerraAsta spaceport in a personal communication in front of only a few trusted people in the palace. Someone must have overheard, or have placed a bug in the reception room.

There was another spy on Alderaan.

Only this spy was more dangerous. This spy was at the palace.

CHAPTER SIXTEEN

Ferus was in his quarters when the signal appeared on the emergency coded channel. Obi-Wan had surfaced at last.

Ferus felt the balled-up frustration of the past days. He didn't bother greeting Obi-Wan. "You *knew* that Leia Organa was the Force-sensitive child!" he spit out at Obi-Wan.

Obi-Wan's lined face was impassive. "Ferus —"

"Don't deny it."

"I'm not denying it."

"You could have saved me a whole lot of trouble! Why did you let me fly blind on this case?"

"I didn't tell you for two reasons. One, I wasn't positive it was Leia Organa. And two, if it was her, the only way I'd know how vulnerable she was would be to let you track her."

Ferus shook his head. "I can't even follow that *sentence,* let alone your reasoning."

"I had to know if there was a spy on Alderaan. The only way to know was for you to follow in his or her footsteps . . . without knowing it."

"Well, let's elect you Minister of Withholding Information, then," Ferus said furiously. "I've been chasing around Aldera like an idiot."

Obi-Wan grinned. Ferus's annoyance grew. That smile of Obi-Wan's — so rare, and then so engaging when it appeared. That hadn't changed.

"Hardly an idiot," Obi-Wan said. "You found out who Leia was. That means she's more vulnerable than I thought. I bet you found the spy who turned her in."

"No thanks to you," Ferus muttered.

"Tell me about Leia," Obi-Wan said unexpectedly. "Is she strong in the Force?"

"It's hard to say," Ferus said. "I didn't pick up anything at first. She definitely has a Force-connection, but without support or training it will likely wither. She will have it, but those around her won't know it. She will be exceptionally quick and bright, perhaps, with fast reflexes. Right now she is vulnerable to being picked up only by another Jedi."

"Or a Sith."

"Or a Sith, yes. As the years pass, this will change."

"Tell me about the spy."

"The spy isn't the problem. My take is that he's a low-level functionary, a spotter. It's clear he's doing it for the money. He has a post overlooking the main spaceport. Probably reports on unusual arrivals and departures. I'm guessing he saw what happened with Leia that morning and reported it because he didn't have anything else to give them. I know he tracked some kind of shipment through the spaceport. But what it is and why, I don't know."

"So what is the problem?"

"There's a mole in the palace. Another spy. Someone close, who Bail trusts."

Obi-Wan let out a breath. "How do you know?"

"Someone reported where Raymus Antilles was going to break his journey at the TerraAsta spaceport. The only ones who knew were Bail's inner circle. A servant could have been listening. He trusts everyone in that place."

"You have to tell him."

"I'm the enemy, remember? Bail doesn't trust me. I have to help him without him knowing that I'm helping him. I can't keep turning up at the palace for no reason. Unless you have a suggestion." Ferus said this last sentence with a twist of irony. So far, Obi-Wan hadn't been much help.

"I'll talk to Bail," Obi-Wan said. "I'll tell him you're on our side. He'll believe me."

"You're going to let Bail know that you're alive?" Ferus asked, surprised.

"He already knows," Obi-Wan said.

Ferus almost threw the comlink against the wall.

"Is there anything else you're not telling me?" he barked.

"There is a great deal," Obi-Wan said, "but it wouldn't help you to know it."

"So you say."

"Go to the palace," Obi-Wan said. "I'll contact Bail."

His reception this time was completely different. Once they were in private, Bail welcomed him warmly, grasping his shoulder as he shook his hand. "You are doing important work," he said. "Those of us who oppose the Empire owe you a debt."

"You put yourself on the line every day in the Senate," Ferus said. "I should be thanking you."

"Come into my study. We can talk with our friend." Bail ushered Ferus into his study. A hologram of Obi-Wan was waiting there. "I sent everyone out of the palace today at Obi-Wan's request," Bail said. "And I upgraded to highest security in my office. Everything we say will be scrambled, coded, and then erased." He turned to Obi-Wan. "Now, my good friend, tell me why you asked for these things."

"Ferus believes that there is a spy in your household," Obi-Wan said.

"Impossible," Bail answered immediately. "Everyone here is either family or friend. Even the servants."

"Even if that's so," Ferus said, "I heard from Hydra that Imperial security knew beforehand that Raymus Antilles would be landing at TerraAsta. It was not a random stop. He was targeted."

"But when I gave Antilles that order, there were only Breha and Deara present," Bail said.

"Someone must have been listening," Ferus said.

Bail shook his head slowly. "I can't believe it."

"You have to believe it," Obi-Wan said. "You have to set a trap for the spy. To have one that close is dangerous not just to you . . ."

"But to Leia as well," Bail said. "Yes, I see that."

"We have to set a trap," Ferus said.

Bail nodded his agreement before turning to Obi-Wan. "I'm glad you contacted me. Something has been on my mind. Have you heard of a group called Moonstrike?"

"Yes," Obi-Wan said. "Ferus has done a few favors for the leader, Flame."

"She contacted me about Alderaan joining the group. Apparently there is to be a first meeting of resistance leaders from planets in the Core. Mon Mothma and I have decided to go very slowly with our resistance efforts. What will be strong must be built with care. But Flame has a different take. Perhaps a better strategy is to strike now, when the Empire is just beginning to consolidate its power. Alderaan is vulnerable. Things are changing so fast. I want to protect my homeworld if I can. If we had alliances willing to help us. . . ." Bail let his voice trail off.

"You are asking my advice?" Obi-Wan asked.

"You are my best counselor," Bail said warmly.

"Ferus and I no doubt disagree on this issue," Obi-Wan said after a pause. "A linkage of resistance movements from planet to planet is of course a goal. The question is timing. Most planets are depleted from the Clone Wars. Empty of weapons, empty of spirit. Bellassa is a rare example of a planet that has managed to mobilize the will of the people to fight the Empire. Most of the others are just glad for peace and hoping for prosperity. To create a full-out rebellion would be difficult if not impossible. In the meantime those resistance leaders who will be needed later will be exposed. So I would advise you not to join Moonstrike. Waiting is hard — but sometimes it is smarter."

"You believe so in this case," Bail said gravely.

"I do."

Ferus saw that Bail was now wavering. That was unfortunate for Flame. He agreed with her that without a political component Moonstrike could be doomed.

Obi-Wan hadn't changed Ferus's mind. It was exactly the opposite. Now he felt more inclined than ever to help Moonstrike.

CHAPTER SEVENTEEN

Revery appeared, a blue planet with a soft haze of pink clouds. Aquamarine seas were visible in a patchwork of gold and green land. It was as lovely from space as it was reputed to be on the surface. Clive entered their coordinates into the nav panel for the mysterious abode of Eve Yarrow.

"Let's just hope we escaped detection. Even if by some miracle Bloomi didn't talk, the report of two bank robbers will be all over the security channel right now."

"Could be," Astri said. Her lips quirked upward. "We'll know soon enough."

Clive gave her a quick glance. "Hey, you *like* this."

"Don't be ridiculous." Astri bent over to fiddle with her utility belt. Her curly hair hid her face.

"You do!" he crowed.

"That's an awful thing to say —"

"I'm not saying you like the Empire. Or that you're glad there was a war so you could go flying through the galaxy with a blaster strapped to your leg. It's just that . . . you're not afraid. You like the adrenaline. You're the one who got us out of that mess back there. So what gives? I thought you were a politician's wife, giving teas and running receptions. Were you some kind of spy back before the Clone Wars?"

"You've got a pretty dumb idea of what a politician's wife does," Astri said, annoyed. "Teas? Receptions? I ran a policy think tank. Until Bog eliminated it after we came up with real solutions to planetary problems."

"You didn't answer my question."

"Before I met Bog — a long time ago — I ran around with the Jedi a bit."

"You ran around with the Jedi? What does that mean?"

"I helped Obi-Wan rescue Qui-Gon. I pretended to be a bounty hunter. Shaved my head. Learned how to shoot a blaster and pilot a swoop. Stuff like that."

"You surprise me, Astri Oddo. Every time I think I know what you're about, you turn out to be about something else."

Astri cocked an eyebrow at him. "That's your flaw, Flax. You don't get it. People aren't about one thing. Now let's keep an eye out. You can't rely on instruments for everything. You need visual sightings. Obi-Wan taught me that."

"I'm guessing there'll be a place to land near the

house," Clive said as the surface of the planet grew closer. "Nobody seems to want neighbors."

It was true. Grand estates were tucked into the mountains many kilometers apart, or displayed on wide spectacular beaches with the mountains behind them. No one had a near neighbor. With coves tucked into steep hills, the geography of the planet cooperated with the need for privacy.

They found the estate they were looking for. Unlike the others, it wasn't on a secluded cove, but tucked into the mountains with a view of the sea below. It was almost invisible from the air. It was more modest than the other places they had passed. Tall trees surrounded it and it was built of the same gray stone of the mountain, so it blended into the slope.

"There's a landing platform and a small hangar," Astri said.

"I don't think there's a big welcome mat," Clive said. "Is there a clear space nearby where we can land?"

Astri studied the nav screen. "Let's try the top of the mountain. We'll have to hike straight down, but at least the cruiser will be hidden."

They found a rocky outcropping to land the cruiser. It was a tough hike down, but they made it to the house, coming down through a steep ravine that left them scratched and bloodied.

Clive trained his electrobinoculars on the hangar.

"There aren't any vehicles inside. Not even an airspeeder."

"Let's get closer."

They moved from tree to tree, inspecting the place. It seemed deserted. Still they were reluctant to move out from the shelter of the trees.

"Look, we have to get closer," Astri said. "We can't stay here all day. We have to risk it."

"If someone's here, I'll say we're lost," Clive said.

"That seems far-fetched."

"I can convince anyone of anything."

"No," Astri said. "You just think you can. Come on."

They left the shelter of the trees and entered the compound. There was no security fence. They simply walked in, finding a path made of smooth flat stones. Astri watched the house but saw no flicker of activity visible behind the large windows.

Alert for trouble, they walked up to the door and knocked.

"There's no security screen," Clive muttered. "This is weird."

"Maybe they're so isolated out here they feel protected," Astri said.

"Well, one thing is for sure," Clive said as the minutes ticked away. "Nobody's home." He reached into his utility belt and removed a small item.

"A rusty coin?" Astri asked. "Are you going to bribe your way in?"

"Not just any coin." Clive held it up. "And it isn't rusty. This is a rare coin from the planet Maill, a thousand years old. Only several hundred were made before they discovered that it had a fatal flaw. The king of Maill had a queen whom he loved. She had hair, they said, the color of a flaming sunset. He used a special alloy of metals to get exactly that hue. Then they discovered that the coin was useless for trade because it was so malleable. Not only that, when heated just a bit it would expand to fill a space and then harden. Ruined many a minting machine before they cancelled the coin. It's the rarest in the galaxy now."

"That's mildly interesting," Astri said, "but what are you going to do with it?"

Instead of answering, Clive also took an ID security card out of his pocket. "Not a real one, a fake one," he explained. "They use a cheaper plastoid. Works better."

Astri stepped back from the door. Clive warmed the coin in his hands, then slid it into the hinge of the security panel. After a moment he was able to slide in the ID security card. The security panel popped open. He studied the circuitry for a moment, then took a small electronic device out of his pocket, attached it, and pressed a sequence of keys. Astri heard a small electronic beep and the door slid open.

"Okay, I'm impressed," she said, before walking in.

"Mildly?" Clive asked as he followed her. "Or extremely?"

The hallway was dark and cool. Astri moved carefully, trying not to make a sound. Her blaster was in her hand now.

They explored the lower floor. The house was furnished in comfortable style, with sleep couches covered in plush fabrics and colorful rugs on the stone floors. The wide windows took in a view of the sea far below. A protocol droid stood inactive in the hallway near the massive front door. The kitchen was stocked with prepared food in the freezer.

"It's just waiting for a visit," Astri said in a whisper. "You could just walk in the door."

"No dust," Clive said. "I wonder if the housekeeping droids are activated on a timer."

Upstairs was a bedroom and a small office. There was no datapad that they could find.

There were several white robes and tunics of varying fabrics hanging in the closet. They could have belonged to a male or female. No clothing was in the drawers.

Clive shook his head. "No information here. If this is Eve Yarrow's house, she doesn't use it much. We can't tie her to Flame or even the Empire if there's nothing here to find."

"Let's look downstairs again," Astri suggested. "If something's here, it won't be in the obvious places."

They returned down to the main level. Clive examined the shelves. He gave a low whistle.

He picked up a dark crystal embedded in a polished stone and held it up. "Look at this." The crystal refracted the dim light in the room and sent shadows skittering on the white walls. "It's the Emperor's Favor."

Astri moved closer, examining the crystal. At first it had looked stark and beautiful, but something about it made her shudder.

"A hunk of rare obsolite crystal embedded in stone from Korriban," Clive explained. He put the object back and rubbed his hands on his tunic. "Given to the chosen of the Empire's elite. Heroes of the Clone Wars. Those who do special favors."

"Very interesting," Astri said. "So Eve Yarrow is in the Empire's elite. She's been rewarded for something."

She turned and continued her examination of the room. Suddenly she stopped and looked at the windows and walls. She paced the room, back and forth. "Something's off," she said. "The dimensions of the room. Looking at it from the mountain . . . there should be another room."

Clive followed her out into the hallway, where Astri pressed her fingers against the wall. "It doesn't make sense," she murmured.

Clive let her explore. Suddenly she crouched down in the hall. She ran her fingers along the wall. She knocked on it. "Here. A hidden room."

Clive joined her. "If you say so. But how do we find it?"

Astri stepped back. Her eyes roamed over the hall-way. Suddenly she sprang forward toward the laser painting of the house that hung on the wall. She tilted it this way and that.

A beam of light shot out from the sun in the painting and hit the opposite wall. Slowly the wall slid back.

"How did you do that?" Clive asked, shaking his head in admiration.

"I heard of using laser paintings as security devices," Astri said. "It's a brand-new system. Top secret from Secure Securities. I learned about it when I was slicing into the main BRT computer on Samaria."

They peered inside the room without entering. It was empty. "A hideout," Clive guessed.

They walked inside.

"If it's a hideout, it's strange that there are no supplies here," Astri said. "There should be food. And a security panel."

"It could be a storage room," Clive said. "Or —"

Suddenly the door slid shut behind them.

He exchanged a glance with Astri. "A trap," he finished.

CHAPTER EIGHTEEN

The meeting with Zan Arbor had gone well. Darth Vader congratulated himself on his approach. Obviously the woman needed incentive. That, and a screaming fast ride in an out-of-control turbolift. He had no doubt that tomorrow he would hear a different tune from her.

And soon the space where Padmé lived inside him would be blank.

His plans were coming together.

His comlink signaled. His Master was calling. Vader felt no unease as he accepted the communication. He had news that would please the Emperor.

"I need a report." It was his Master's most severe tone.

"We have made *progress*, my Master," Vader said. "Twilight is ready. Phase One is already in motion."

"*Good. Good.* And Alderaan?"

"The Imperial Governor arrives tomorrow. Our contact assures us that all is in place."

"Then, my young apprentice, return to Alderaan. Your work is there for now."

"Yes, Master." He had to obey, of course. But he would have to find time to corner Zan Arbor again before he left. He wanted to be sure that she would have the memory agent on-line soon. Ferus Olin couldn't touch him with a lightsaber. He must not be allowed to touch him with his memories. They were far more dangerous.

CHAPTER NINETEEN

Keets, Curran, and Dex huddled together at the safe house in Thugger's Alley. They had spent hours on communications back and forth between various groups on various planets, trying to reach an agreement for a meeting. Things were far from settled.

"I think we'd better shut down communications, at least for awhile," Dex said. "We've already pushed our limit. Any more and we risk some Imperial scanner picking up increased activity for this sector."

Keets nodded. "I wish —"

Suddenly Dex whipped his repulsorlift chair around. "We've got trouble, my boys," he said.

For a half of a moment they stood transfixed, staring at the security screens. The alley was under attack. Squads of stormtroopers charged through while the air overhead was thick with small-range armed artillery cruisers and swoops.

"They're landing on the roofs," Keets said, swallowing. He couldn't quite believe it was happening. Not yet.

"You know the drill, boys," Dex said. "We've prepared for this day. I'll see you at the tunnel."

Keets and Curran tried not to look at the security screens as they methodically wiped all the datapads and computers. They knew they had only seconds to finish the job. They fused the circuitry so that all the communication and storage would be not only inoperable but impossible to trace. It was too late to warn away anyone who might be in the vicinity, but they knew the Imperial presence was so large that the surrounding populace of the Orange District would spread the word quickly.

Dex had gone to wipe his research library, a task that sickened him. He had spent years amassing information, and now it would be gone in a moment. It contained beings and planets and possible scenarios for revolt on different planets as well as information on systems, cities, minerals, mines, out of the way spaceports, cantinas where one could be sure to be left alone. It was too dangerous to download it onto a chip; he knew the likelihood of capture despite all his precautions. At least some of it was in his head.

Months before, Dex had prepared for the move to the Orange District with his usual thoroughness. He had checked the old maps and read the old histories. Then he had blasted with some extremely discreet explosive through his own floor and used sensor equipment to figure out how to tap into an ancient alley that had once intersected with Thugger's Alley. Dex had spent long days down below ground with Oryon the Bothan and whichever stray member of the Erased he could corral for a day's work. They'd managed to dig their way with a converted version of a mole miner, through the rock into what remained of the ancient alley. He knew that they'd never make it out through Thugger's Alley or off the roof. The tunnel would have to save them.

Dex met the others in the hallway, which was already filled with smoke.

"Bad news," Curran said. His forehead was shiny with sweat and his long thick hair had come loose from its metal coil. It lay in tangles down his back.

"They blasted through the roof," Keets explained. His face was gray with dust. "Used too much explosive. The debris blocks our access to the turbolift. We'll have to come at it from the other wing of the house."

They all exchanged glances. This was a worst-case scenario, one they hadn't planned for. The only route to escape meant they'd have to take the hallway that ran along the front of the house. They could get caught between the stormtroopers entering from the roof and those entering from the front. They wouldn't stand a chance.

"Let's get moving then," Dex said.

The safe house had been designed to confound pursuers, with false walls and twisting passageways too narrow for major weaponry. Still they could hear the stormtroopers uncomfortably close. They were charging down the hallways behind them and blasting down doors. They could hear them searching the rooms and the muffled sound of their communications.

"If they get through that armored door downstairs in the next minute we could be in trouble," Dex said.

The blast sent shock waves against their ears. The house gave a great shudder and almost seemed to lift up and settle back down.

"They're in," Keets said.

They heard the stormtroopers charging up the stairs. Dex hit a button on his repulsorlift chair.

They heard the sound of scrambling, then bodies hitting the ground. The amplified groans and shouts came to them faintly.

"Flipped the stairs into ramp mode," Dex told them. "It will buy us a minute."

"We need more than a minute," Keets said, drawing his blaster.

One more hallway. One last burst of speed to get to the hidden turbolift.

The stormtroopers behind them were so close they could hear the headset communications now.

Nothing so far.

Use explosives on the walls. They could be hiding behind them. Not too much this time! The house is unstable.

Continue on northeast quadrant. Meet up with squadron three-six-ten.

Curran turned the last corner and saw stormtroopers spilling up the ramp, climbing over the bodies of their comrades who had fallen when Dex suddenly eliminated the stairs. Curran and Keets let loose with blasterfire. Energy bolts streaked through the smoky air.

The stormtroopers returned fire. Keets dived and rolled, still shooting. His main objective was to protect Dex, who could make that repulsorlift chair travel, but couldn't maneuver it to escape a barrage of blasterfire. Curran kept himself between the stormtroopers and Dex.

"Run, you two! Run!" Dex thundered. "Leave me here! We agreed!"

Weeks before, Dex had told them that if they were invaded, he was the most vulnerable. Because of his bulk, he simply couldn't move fast enough if the worst happened. He had extracted a promise from Keets and Curran that they would escape if they could and leave him behind. He had forced them to agree. It was best if at least a few of them were able to escape. Dex had told them that he'd led a long life, "sometimes a scoundrel's life, but a good one," and he was ready to give up his life if he had to. "But you boys, you have a long way to go," he'd told them.

Yes, they'd given their word. But Keets and Curran knew even without exchanging a glance that they couldn't leave Dex behind.

The blasterfire was so thick that the air seemed full of dancing light. Keets saw a blaster bolt hit Dex, who slumped over. Shouting at Curran to cover him, he leaped on the chair and pushed the velocity. The chair shot forward, straight into an advancing line of stormtroopers.

Screaming with rage, Keets blasted through the line and kept going. Curran hooked an arm around the chair and pulled himself onto the back of the chair, which lurched but kept on. Dex was half-conscious as Keets pushed the speed, whizzing down the corridor through the smoke. The last burst of blasterfire hit the repulsorlift engine. They heard a small explosion and the chair began to buck and slow.

Curran threw himself at the hidden panel and activated it. They only had seconds now. The stormtroopers were making their way down the twisting hallway. The panel slid up and Keets pushed the chair inside. Dex's head lolled and his six arms hung limply at his sides. Keets didn't know if he was alive or dead.

Curran hit the sensor. "Close!" he begged the panel.

It shut before the stormtroopers rounded the corner. The turbolift zoomed down. The doors opened on the damp, cool, tunnel.

Pushing and pulling, they got Dex out of the turbolift.

"There's an airspeeder down here we can use," Curran said. "We'll have to leave the chair."

Keets peered at Dex anxiously. Was he . . .

Dex opened one eye. "You gave me your word," he muttered.

Keets could see the great effort it cost him to speak. He leaned closer to Dex's ear. "Since when is my word worth anything, you monkey lizard? You should have known better."

An explosion above caused the tunnel to shudder, and dirt rained down on them.

Dex winced, but Keets saw the light in his eyes. He would make it. "What are you waiting for then, boys? Get me out of here."

CHAPTER TWENTY

Trever and Ry-Gaul stood back as Linna and Tobin embraced. Linna laid her head along her husband's chest. They had been separated for too long. Trever turned away to give them privacy. He hadn't seen that kind of love since his parents were alive. He didn't like to be reminded. It made an empty place in him that he usually was able to fill up with other things. Friends, food, danger, wondering what his next move would be.

Finally they moved apart. They came toward Ry-Gaul and Trever, holding hands.

"Thank you," Tobin said. Linna smiled. Trever had never realized that she was beautiful. She had always looked so sad and strained.

They had met Tobin on a hidden landing platform close to the Orange District. Surrounded by airspeeders, they huddled together. The thick traffic in the spacelanes overhead was beginning to blink and blur with the first lights of evening.

"There is a space cruiser here for you to use," Ry-Gaul said. "Do you need a safe destination?"

"There's a place we know," Tobin said, with a glance at Linna. "A place we were happy once. On Mila."

Ry-Gaul nodded. "Not too much Imperial activity in that quadrant. I included fresh ID docs in the cruiser."

"They sent me to Despayre," Tobin said. "They separated all the scientists. We were not allowed to speak to others with different areas of knowledge. I was kept with the structural engineers. But I know there were weapons-delivery technicians and systems scientists. Chemists. It's a huge effort to build . . . something. Something terrible."

Ry-Gaul nodded. "I'll tell Ferus."

Linna held out her hand. She pressed a small bundle into Ry-Gaul's hand. "I don't want this," she said quietly. "It is the only thing left from that terrible experiment. The documentation and the memory agent itself. Zan Arbor's records have been destroyed, as well as her mind. I suggest you destroy this, too."

Ry-Gaul was the most reserved guy Trever had ever met. It surprised him when Ry-Gaul stepped forward and embraced first Linna, then Tobin. He did it without the awkwardness Trever would expect from him.

"You saved our lives," Linna said. "We'll never forget that."

"You saved mine once," Ry-Gaul said. "We are now bound together by the stars and by the Force. If you need me, I will come."

Ry-Gaul and Trever waited until the star cruiser shot off into the space lane. They stayed even though after a moment they couldn't distinguish the lights of the cruiser from any of the others in the heavy Coruscant traffic.

"I've been saying good-bye an awful lot these days," Trever said. "It never gets easier somehow."

"No," Ry-Gaul said with his customary terseness.

"Well, I think I'm done for awhile," Trever said.

They walked the rest of the way to the Orange District. As they descended in a series of turbolifts to the district, they didn't speak. Sadness hung on both of them.

As they neared the district the turbolifts stopped working. They were usually sabotaged as soon as they were fixed. They walked down ramps and through the narrow alleys and streets toward Thugger's Alley. It was dark now, and the orange-colored lights threw deep shadows. As they got closer, Ry-Gaul's pace suddenly quickened.

"The streets are almost empty," he said. "Something's wrong."

Trever had to trot to keep up with him. His heart began to hammer. He could smell something now, and he knew Ry-Gaul could too.

"Smoke," Trever said.

They began to run. They turned the last corner and saw . . . nothing.

The labyrinth of Thugger's Alley had been destroyed. There was nothing left. Not a wall, not a piece of stone. It had been vaporized. The ground still smoked.

"Dex," Trever croaked. "Keets. Curran . . ."

"Come," Ry-Gaul said, tugging on Trever's arm. Trever couldn't move.

Ry-Gaul had to lead him away. There was always the danger of spies waiting to see who would turn up.

Expertly Ry-Gaul led him through the back alleys until they reached an area where the accustomed crowds were milling in the cafes and loitering outside noisy, dim restaurants. Trever felt shocked to the core. He put one foot in front of the other but he wasn't aware of walking. With every step a name chimed in his head. Dex. Curran. Keets.

And who else had been there? Flame? Oryon still dropped in from time to time, although he was spending most of his time on the asteroid now. And what about Solace? You never knew where she'd turn up. . . .

"Flame," Ry-Gaul said quietly.

At first Trever was confused. Ry-Gaul just seemed to echo the name in his mind. Then he realized that Ry-Gaul had spotted her.

Relief washed through Trever. They made their way to Flame, who was sitting outside a café, an untouched mug of tea in front of her. Trever saw that her hands were shaking.

Her face cleared when she saw Trever. "You're safe," she said, rising and hugging him.

"As you are," Ry-Gaul said. His silver-gray eyes rested on her face intently.

"I don't know what happened to the others," she said. "I wasn't there. But . . . the word on the street is that everyone is dead. They didn't capture anyone. They searched every dwelling and then blew up the whole alley. No one could have survived."

"What do we do now?" Trever asked, trying to swallow his grief and shock, although he knew he wouldn't be able to. It sat like a rock inside his stomach and choked his every breath.

Ry-Gaul sat down heavily in a chair next to Flame. "We go on."

CHAPTER TWENTY-ONE

Bail still refused to believe that anyone living at the palace could be a spy, but after upgrading his system for the holo-communication with Obi-Wan, he picked up a bug. Someone had invaded his system and placed a monitor on it.

"Luckily it doesn't appear that my code has been broken . . . yet," Bail said. "But the record of who I contact can be just as damaging. I wiped our communication with Obi-Wan, of course, but everything that came before has no doubt been reported."

"The only other people who knew that Antilles would go through TerraAsta were Queen Breha and Deara," Ferus said. He hesitated. "Deara . . ."

"Don't." Bail's voice was curt. "She is closest to us. Breha's sister. Her loyalty is unquestioned."

"You said Memily was a new employee," Ferus said.

"She is the daughter of one of my most trusted friends."

"Senator Organa, *someone* has to be the spy."

Bail sighed and said nothing.

"We have to set a trap," Ferus said. "It's the only way. Someone here at the palace is passing along information to Dartan Ziemba. Look, I know that you've been fighting a losing battle to keep an Imperial Governor off your planet."

"I've lost that battle. He arrives tomorrow." Bail shook his head. "Deara tells me that there are some who want me to offer armed resistance. Buy weapons. That would violate everything we stand for."

"I saw Deara at the market at dawn yesterday," Ferus said. "Does she go often?"

Bail crossed and looked out the window. His thoughts seemed far away. He waved a hand. "Lately, yes. She brings back fresh muffins for the children."

Why? Ferus wondered. When Memily was such a good baker?

Ferus thought again of meeting Deara at the market. He had been distracted. Searching for the spy, and thinking about his own use of anger, how he had tapped into the dark side of the Force and what that meant.

He hadn't thought it through.

"I have to go," he told Bail.

"Now? What about setting the trap?"

"If I'm right, I'll come back with a plan," Ferus promised.

* * *

Ferus walked through the market. He saw Dartan Ziemba down the first lane of stalls. Dartan sold children's toys. Ferus kept out of sight, watching him. Business wasn't too good.

He kept walking, up and down, watching and looking, pretending to study goods, occasionally buying a thing or two to avoid suspicion. It was a pleasant day and the market was crowded.

When he had discovered what he'd come for, he hurried back to the palace, slashing the airspeeder through the space lanes. There was no time to lose.

He burst into Bail's office. "You must write a secret memo saying that Alderaan will meet the Governor with armed resistance!"

"Why would I do that? Alderaan has no weapons."

"I'm afraid that you do. Dartan Ziemba was the conduit. Mostly likely someone from the Empire — I suspect Darth Vader — arranged for a shipment of weapons to arrive at the spaceport. Ziemba was to arrange to hide them and then move them to another location at the right time."

"Where?"

"The open-air market."

"I'm not getting this," Bail said. "Why would Vader want to arm Alderaan?"

"He doesn't. He wants to send the Imperial Governor here and expose the weapons so he has a reason to place your planet under his control."

Bail nodded. "Of course. That is exactly the way he thinks."

"But if you send that message — that you will meet the Governor with armed resistance — it will go to the Emperor himself. They will be delighted that you've fallen in with their plans without even knowing it. You've been told that your people *want* you to fight —"

Bail looked ashen. "By Deara."

"And so they will arrive here with weapons and ships, and they will find . . . nothing. Because we're going to get those weapons out. You're going to detain Ziemba for questioning and then let him go. Meanwhile, the market will be cleaned of weapons. Then when the Empire arrives they'll meet no resistance. They'll look like fools. The people of Alderaan will be the heroes. And the spy will be discredited. His information will be suspect. Not only his information on you, but his information on Leia. "

"That's diabolical," Bail said. "I like it. As long as my people don't get hurt."

"The Empire will bring Star Destroyers to scare you," Ferus said. "But they won't attack."

Bail stood. "Then I have work to do."

Hydra closed the holofile. She looked at Ferus.

"You intend to submit this?"

"I do," Ferus said.

"You have reached the conclusion that the report of a Force-sensitive child is without foundation?"

"I have."

"Well, I have not reached that conclusion."

"We've conducted dozens of interviews. Combed through official records. Examined the site. Done surveillance. It's clear to me that whatever happened wasn't noteworthy. Not an example of the Force, but a coincidence so unremarkable that . . . nobody remarked on it."

"There is a reason nobody is talking to us."

"Sure," Ferus said. "They hate us."

Hydra batted her hand at his words as if they were a cloud of tiny flies. "That is immaterial. They're hiding something."

"They are afraid of us," Ferus said. "With good reason. So they aren't going to give us any information. But let's not confuse that with actually having something to say. I say we close the file. I'm your superior," Ferus reminded her.

She hesitated. "Technically that is true."

"Is it true, or not true?" Ferus asked the question brusquely. If he pushed her, Hydra would push back. Her contempt for him would guarantee that.

Because he had to discredit her as well as Dartan Ziemba.

On the way, he'd tried to reach Keets at Thugger's Alley. He wanted Keets to pull in some favors with the renegade journalists who were starting up the Shadow Net, the alternative to the Empire-controlled news. The lack of response from Keets or anyone at the hideout on Thugger's Alley was worrisome.

"It is true." Her mouth set angrily. "And it is also true that in cases where Inquisitors do not agree, the junior member of the team may write a dissenting report."

"Certainly. If you feel you have a solid foundation, despite investigating for four days and coming up empty-handed, then feel free to clutter the Imperial archives with another memo." Ferus shrugged. "Have fun. But I suggest we move onto the next names on the list and really get something done. It's time to leave Alderaan."

Hydra's usually expressionless eyes burned with fury. "I'll file my report immediately."

Good, Ferus thought.

"Soon Alderaan will know how fruitless it is to resist," she said. "They'll recognize that we're in charge. Investigations like this will then go smoothly. The Imperial Governor will see to that."

He wanted to smile at her smugness. Instead he nodded gravely. "Yes," he said. "I wish for that too."

CHAPTER TWENTY-TWO

Breha and Bail waited in their sitting room for Deara. Bail looked at his wife's lovely face. He could see the pain there. He had broken her heart.

Her beloved sister was a spy.

He had written the message and put a false "send" on it. He had set the new security control. He had seen with his own eyes on the monitor that Deara had sneaked into his office, copied his message, and sent it off.

He placed his hand over his wife's. The burden of ruling was on Breha every moment of her life. She had loved Bail through many separations where she would remain at the palace and he would be at the Senate on Coruscant. She had encouraged his political career. She had worried about him during the Clone Wars. And even while she ruled her world and watched out for its citizens, she had drawn her family close, had extended a hand to all her family, her friends, down to the last citizen of Alderaan, she was there to fight for them and help them and represent them. Now this.

Deara entered, her face surrounded by thick coils of lustrous dark hair. She had her usual warm smile. "It's a lovely day. How about having lunch in the garden?"

"Deara, we need to speak with you," Breha said.

Breha's tone made Deara stop short. "Is something wrong?"

"Something is very wrong. There is a spy in the house."

Deara swallowed. "I see."

"You are that spy."

Bail admired how Breha kept her focus. She didn't let one bit of her anguish show.

They didn't know what Deara would do. They had expected her to deny it. But there was no defiance. No argument. Deara merely crumpled. She sank onto the floor, her face in her hands.

No one said anything for long moments. Breha kept her gaze on her sister. "He came to me when I was visiting Coruscant." Deara's voice was muffled.

"Vader?"

Slowly, she nodded. "He threatened me. He was terrifying. Then he said he just wanted . . . to know when Bail was here, and when he was planning to leave. At first. Then he wanted . . . more."

"You gave them information about my private communications," Bail said.

She nodded tearfully. "Just who you wrote to, who had sent you messages. Not what was in them."

"Only because you could not break the code."

"No!" she protested, vigorously shaking her head. "I would never have told them that much. I thought the information I gave would be harmless. . . ."

"You told them that Raymus Antilles would be returning through the TerraAsta spaceport," Bail said. "He could have been arrested."

"They had no reason to arrest him," Deara said. "They wanted to discover if he was carrying a message. I knew your code was unbreakable —"

"These are merely excuses for the inexcusable!" Bail thundered, suddenly losing his temper.

Breha shot Bail a look to keep his voice down. They would do this with their dignity intact. "You told us there were those who wanted to use weapons against the Empire," she said. "Was that true?"

Deara shook her head and said through her tears, "I was told to say it. I knew you would discount it! It seemed such a small thing. . . ." She cried harder.

"What about Leia?" Breha asked. "You filed a report about her. Was that a small thing?"

"It wasn't me! I would never inform on Leia," Deara insisted. "I would never endanger the children."

"Deara, don't you see that you already have?" Breha

asked her. "By becoming a spy, you brought danger to this house."

Deara shook her head tearfully. "My dear sister, there is already danger in this house. Bail's opposition to the Emperor has placed you there, not me."

Breha looked at Bail. She knew those words had gone to his heart. It was his greatest fear, that his work in the Senate would one day threaten his family.

"How dare you say that! My husband's courage fills my heart with pride. He does not bring danger to this house. He brings honor to it. You are the one who brought dishonor and danger here."

Bail took Breha's hand and kissed it. She turned to him with tears in her eyes. "Dangerous days," she said softly. "But we will never, ever lose our resolve."

A cowed Deara put her hands over her face again. "I'm so sorry."

"You are weak," Breha said. "But you are my sister. You must leave the palace forever."

Deara nodded, her face hidden by her hands.

"We have arranged secret passage for you, and a safehouse on Ankori-7," Bail said.

She lifted her face, surprised. "I am free to go?"

"Yes," Breha said. "You are free to go."

"You let her go?" Ferus asked, incredulous. "You had an opportunity. She could have fed them more information! You could have used her."

"She is family," Breha said.

"At the very least, she deserved prison," Ferus said.

"She is family," Breha repeated softly.

"You could be putting yourself in danger," Ferus said. "They could track her down. They could still use her."

"If I make a mistake, I'd rather do it on the side of forgiveness," Bail said.

To this, Ferus had no answer. The Holocron burned inside his tunic and he knew what the voice would say.

It is foolish not to destroy your enemies. Foolish and cowardly.

But Ferus looked with his heart at Bail and Breha, and thought they were among the bravest people he'd ever known.

There was too much heartbreak in the galaxy now. Too many families broken, too many friends torn apart.

What would it be like to never feel heartbreak again? What if you could conquer grief, tamp it down, and never feel the searing heat of it again?

You can.

Ferus felt the heat of the Holocron next to his chest. Suddenly his breath was short. Perspiration broke out all over his body.

All of that, and more, can be yours as easily as saying one word.

Yes.

CHAPTER
TWENTY-THREE

Bail and Ferus waited at the spaceport. It was what they had expected, but it was still a terrifying sight to see the inner atmosphere thick with Imperial craft. The Governor's star cruiser was flanked with Imperial fighters.

"I hate this," Bail said, his teeth set.

"Are the reporters in place?" Ferus asked.

Bail nodded. "The Shadow Net will have a simultaneous broadcast of the arrival," he said. "The news will be all over the Core."

"They'll take their time landing for maximum effect," Ferus said. Then he slipped away; it would not benefit either of them for him and Bail to be seen together.

The first ship to land was a transport ship. The stormtroopers poured out, their weapons held high. They lined up in long rows, sunlight glinting on the white plastoid.

All traffic had been halted for the arrival. The Alderaanians at the spaceport were crowded behind the bristling weapons of the stormtroopers.

The Imperial Governor's star cruiser landed.

The ramp descended. Another squad of stormtroopers came trotting down, their weapons extended as if expecting to meet a battle.

They were followed by a small man in a purple cape — the Imperial Governor. Next to him was Emperor Palaptine. A shudder went through the crowd. From a distance, Ferus could see Bail stiffen. They hadn't expected to see Palpatine himself.

"People of Alderaan," the Governor called out, his voice loud, reaching every person at the spaceport. "We come in peace. We are here to protect you. Word has reached our ears that you are prepared to fight. We do not wish a confrontation. The Empire is about peace."

Bail stepped forward. "The galaxy knows that Alderaan is peaceful. We have no weapons."

The Emperor signaled to his elite Red Guards. "We shall see."

The procession moved to the open-air market below. Customers and vendors ran as the stormtroopers methodically overturned stalls and bins full of items. Fruit was trampled underfoot. The ground was soon stained red from berries.

The stormtroopers uncovered the durasteel bins.

"Open them," the Governor commanded.

The stormtroopers opened every bin in the market. They were filled with tools. Handmade clothes. Fabric. Kitchen items. The stuff of everyday living, nothing more.

The vendors had worked all night to get the weapons out. Raymus Antilles had loaded them aboard his cruiser secretly and took off. Once again, there were no weapons on Alderaan.

The Imperial Governor stood by the Emperor's side, surrounded by hundreds of troops. The market was wrecked. The people stood, watching. Not afraid, Ferus saw. Smiling.

It was the sight of the Emperor surrounded by ruined fruit, by squads of stormtroopers facing off against a threat that consisted of children and ordinary citizens out with their shopping baskets. It was the sight of the Imperial Governor, so slight and small, with his ornate purple cape and bodyguards with raised rifles around him. On Alderaan, the sight did not make sense.

A slow rumble began in the crowd. It started with barely concealed smiles, then erupted into titters and laughter.

The Imperial Governor looked up at the Emperor nervously. The stormtroopers looked for an order.

"Disperse!" the Governor rasped. "Back to the transports!"

Ferus smiled. So did the Emperor.

He felt the wind stir his cheek. Darth Vader was suddenly beside him.

"I see this amuses you," he said.

"All of this effort for one little Governor," Ferus said. "Why the show of force? There's no resistance on Alderaan."

"Resistance is everywhere," Vader said. "It is up to us to decide when and where to crush it. You gave these people a hollow victory."

"I had nothing to do with it."

"So you say. Their defeat will come. This humiliation will not be forgotten. The Empire chooses its time. Yesterday on Coruscant we became tired of observing a resistance cell right under our noses. So we crushed it."

"Good for you," Ferus said, but his anxiety ticked inside him.

"Thugger's Alley, in the Orange District," Vader continued. "You might have known the one in charge — he had been friendly with the Jedi. Dexter Jettster, his name was."

"Was?"

"His hideout was destroyed. Everyone inside was killed."

Shock and grief tore through him. But now was not the time. It was time to hit Vader back. "When I mentioned Mustafar to you the other day, I fear I upset you."

The Dark Lord must have been prepared for him to

bring it up. He didn't give off any ripple of concern. "Save your fears for *yourself*," he said instead.

It happened instantaneously. Ferus felt as though the top of his head had blown off. It was immediate and visceral. Every clue clicked into place, every suspicion, every nagging sense that he was missing something important.

They had stood outside the council room together.

"I'm afraid for you. You think admitting you were wrong opens you up to attack," Ferus had said. He still felt shell-shocked and strange from his conference with the Jedi Masters. He still couldn't believe that he had just resigned from the Jedi Order.

Anakin's lip had curled. "I think you should save your fears for yourself."

Darth Vader was Anakin Skywalker.

He didn't know *how* he knew it, but he knew it.

Reeling, Ferus stood next to Vader as the Emperor approached them. Clouds had rolled in like a great gray carpet; a storm was brewing. The thickness of the air and the coming storm seemed to give a hard charge to the atmosphere.

Ferus felt the blast of the Emperor's fury, though he remained calm. Palpatine came straight to Vader.

"A trap," he said. He looked over at the people, who were now turning away, and added in a terrifying whisper, "I could kill them all, if I *wanted*."

"There is nothing stopping you, Master," Vader said.

"You should *remember* that we are being monitored. Someday, yes. Not now."

Darth Vader said nothing. Ferus began to enjoy himself. He'd never been present while Vader was rebuked by his Master.

Anakin had always hated being chided in public.

Anakin had always wanted to be the best.

Use it. Use what you know. Bring him down. He is half of what he was.

As if the Emperor had heard the voice as well, he turned to Ferus. The heat left his voice. "But you have done your job *well*," he said.

Ferus felt Vader's frustration build. If Vader unleashed it, Ferus wondered if he could tear the spaceport apart.

The Emperor smiled.

"It is time for you to take a second-in-command, *Lord Vader*," he said, chuckling. "And I think Ferus Olin is perfect for the job."